OTHER
Harlequin Romances
by IRIS DANBURY

The Scented Island

by

IRIS DANBURY

Harlequin Books

TORONTO • LONDON • NEW YORK • AMSTERDAM • SYDNEY • WINNIPEG

Original hardcover edition published in 1976
by Mills & Boon Limited

ISBN 0-373-02042-2

Harlequin edition published February 1977

Printed in U.S.A.

CHAPTER ONE

'Is it a good holiday?'

Lexa glanced up at the man who had asked her this question. 'The best I've ever had,' she answered with conviction. 'I've not usually been able to afford anything as far afield as Corsica. And never, of course, three weeks at a time. I'm really grateful to you, Clifford, for arranging it.'

They were stretched out in adjacent lounge chairs and now Clifford leaned towards her to pat her hand companionably. 'There'll be plenty of exciting holidays in the future,' he promised.

In this lovely garden Lexa gave herself up drowsily to rosy dreams of the future. Clifford was an ambitious young barrister climbing rapidly in his profession, and Lexa wondered sometimes how she had managed to attract his attention when he must know so many other girls, prettier, more talented, more sophisticated.

Lexa had met him through her aunt with whom she lived at Walton-upon-Thames. Aunt Beatrice, connected with various local committees, hobnobbed with half the neighbourhood ladies, among them Mrs Howent, Clifford's mother. A Christmas party at the Howents' had led to this quite firm friendship between Lexa and Clifford. He took her to occasional dances, to tennis parties, for lazy afternoons boating on the river, and most mornings he gave her a lift in his car as far as Kingston, where she worked in a department store.

Until recently she had been happy working in the piano and record department, but a take-over by a larger company resulted in alterations by the management.

'We're closing down on pianos and musical instruments, except guitars, Miss Merton,' she had been told, 'and extending more into pop records and cassettes.'

To Lexa this was a disappointment, for she had studied

5

music since she was a child and had passed her examinations up to teaching standard. Her ambition had always been to become a concert pianist, but she knew she would never rise to that height, nor was the money available for her training. Aunt Beatrice had provided her with a home after Lexa's parents had died, and was not particularly well off.

For a time she settled down in the newly-organised department, although she missed the opportunity to demonstrate pianos to potential customers by playing part of a Chopin valse or a Liszt Hungarian dance.

A couple of months ago, the assistant manager interviewed her again and informed her that a brisk young man was to be put in charge of her department.

'We feel that you're not really interested in anything except the classical stuff, so we're transferring you to Gloves and Scarves, where we hope you'll be happier.'

Lexa would have preferred to refuse outright and give in her notice immediately, but it was hardly fair to deprive her aunt of her contribution to the housekeeping expenses.

'I'll try it for a while,' she agreed, with the mental reservation that she would look out for something more congenial.

When she told Clifford of these setbacks, he was sympathetic. 'You ought to leave that glorified drapers' shop,' he advised. 'I could find you a most satisfying job in a solicitors' office in Chancery Lane. You do know shorthand and typing, don't you?'

'Of course.'

'Well then, that's settled. You tell me when you want to leave and I'll arrange it all.'

Aunt Beatrice approved the idea. 'If you and Clifford eventually get married, at least you'll understand all the legal terms and know what he's talking about. You might prove to be a great help to him.'

'We're not really engaged yet,' Lexa reminded her aunt. 'It's only a vague sort of understanding.' She was not foolish enough to imagine that a few outings or being escorted to dances automatically led to marriage and, in all fairness,

Clifford had never mentioned marriage or indicated his ultimate intentions.

Then he surprised Lexa one evening. 'I've had an invitation to Corsica,' he told her. 'I have friends there, the Franklands. I met them in London last year, when Edgar Frankland was involved in a legal dispute. They're interesting people. He's a composer——'

'Edgar Frankland? Oh, I've heard of him,' Lexa said quickly. 'He's written a symphony and some quartets, probably other works I don't know about.'

'His wife, Marguerite, is French, plays the cello,' continued Clifford, 'and she has a daughter who I'm told is a genius on the violin. So you should be happy in such a musical world.'

Before leaving, Lexa had given in her notice at the store and then taken a short refresher course to polish up her shorthand and typewriting. It would never do to let Clifford down by being incompetent in a post to which he had recommended her.

So for the past fortnight, she had revelled in the holiday atmosphere of the Franklands' beautiful old house and rambling gardens in the south-west corner of Corsica. The grey stone house, called Fontenay, was L-shaped, the older part tall and four-storeyed, for Corsicans always built their houses like small forts with good look-outs from the attics. Additions had been made by successive owners, then a two-storey wing extending along one side. The *maquis*, the thicket of perfumed bushes, juniper and myrtle, arbutus and rosemary, began only a short distance from the house, as though the latter had been built in a clearing and now the maquis was determined to encroach again. Many of the bushes were in flower and the hillsides were dotted with splashes of colour, mauve and white, yellow and blue. Beyond the bush-covered hills rose a majestic range of mountains, saw-toothed towering walls streaked with vertical crevasses.

A path led down through the trees to a small sandy beach where the scented bushes flowed down almost to ground level and the shore was edged with small grey-leaved plants with bright golden flowers.

As Lexa had already assured Clifford, the holiday had been ideal. There had been trips to various parts of the island, dancing and dining in Ajaccio, drives to Bonifacio or up through the mountains. Clifford preferred long, lazy afternoons on one of the uncrowded sandy beaches or walks through the pinewoods and, since she was indebted to him for bringing her here, Lexa agreed, although privately she wanted to explore every part, every village or coastal bay of this fascinating island. The chance might never come again, she reflected.

As far as the evenings were concerned, she had been perhaps even happier spending them at home in the Franklands' long drawing room than out in a smart café. Edgar, a quiet man in his early fifties, discussed musical topics with her, and she accompanied Marguerite in cello pieces or trios with Gabrielle, Marguerite's sixteen-year-old daughter, who promised to be a brilliant violinist.

The remaining member of the Frankland family, Bryden, Edgar's own son by a former marriage, was rarely at home, and even when present declared he had little interest in music as such—'except for a jolly good tune'. Edgar explained that Bryden looked after the family property in various parts of the island.

'My father owns a couple of hotels,' Bryden told her rather brusquely one evening. 'Several oddments of holiday accommodation, as well. Someone must give attention to material matters. We can't all have our heads in the clouds and be concerned with crotchets and quavers.'

His tone on that occasion had given Lexa the impression that he considered musical subjects trivial and a waste of valuable time.

Now more than a fortnight of Lexa's holiday had sped by and only another few days remained. Marguerite had given several small parties or dinners so that Clifford and Lexa could meet other young people in the neighbourhood and among them, Philippe Moriani and his sister Suzanne seemed to be the most frequent guests, for they lived only about a mile away.

8

Sometimes Philippe arranged a foursome with his sister and took Clifford and Lexa to little-known villages or showed them a breathtaking viewpoint from a hilltop.

Lexa knew that the Morianis were coming to dinner tonight. 'Gabrielle told me that they live with their father in a very dilapidated old villa and that's why they don't usually entertain in their own home. They take people out to restaurants instead.'

'Could be,' agreed Clifford sleepily. 'Philippe mentioned a trip tomorrow to the Marmano forest and then to a place called Vizzavona in the centre of the island. I don't think we've been there.'

'I shall look forward to that,' she said.

Clifford gave her an amused glance. 'The trip? Or being with Philippe?'

She smiled back. 'Both, probably.'

'He's a handsome devil, certainly, but perhaps not to be trusted.'

'Why?' demanded Lexa. 'Have you weighed him up as if he were a witness in one of your courts?'

'No, not yet. But if he were a witness on the opposite side, I'd do my best to punch holes in his tale.'

Lexa laughed. 'Poor Philippe! He'd have a bad time with you.'

'Now, Bryden, he's altogether a different sort of fish,' continued Clifford musingly. 'Straight and honest as they come. Whatever he said, one would be inclined to believe him.'

As Lexa had met Bryden only on the two or three occasions when he had been at home, she was unable to make an assessment.

At dinner that evening, in between the snippets of conversation, she gave more attention to the other guests. There was Philippe opposite her, handsome, dark-eyed, a slightly hawk nose that acknowledged his Corsican parentage. His father, Gregorio, was proud of his true Corsican ancestry, but he had married a French wife from whom Suzanne undoubtedly inherited her shining blonde hair and delicate features.

9

Gabrielle, Marguerite's daughter by her former marriage, was small, dark and alert, and Lexa hoped most intensely that the girl's dreams of becoming a famous violinist would come true. Lexa herself was taller than either of the other girls, with bronze shoulder-length hair and hazel eyes.

Lastly, of the young people, there remained Bryden Frankland, who had returned this afternoon after an absence of several days. Surreptitiously, Lexa contrasted him with Clifford. Both men were tall and broad-shouldered, but their colouring differed. Clifford's fair hair, blue eyes and a certain roundness of feature hinted at an affability of character speedily belied in the law courts, as many wrong-doers had found to their cost.

Bryden's dark brown hair, grey eyes, tanned, almost gaunt features, added up to a sombre expression, particularly when one glanced at the usually unsmiling mouth. Comparing the two men, Lexa decided that a girl would always be more comfortable in the company of Clifford than that of Bryden. There was something vaguely unsettling about Bryden's demeanour, as though he were constantly sizing up other people and finding them worthless.

The talk at the dinner table now concerned the projected trip tomorrow.

'We must make an early start,' suggested Philippe, giving Lexa a questioning glance.

'How early?' she queried.

'Shall we say six o'clock?' he hazarded.

'We'll not say anything of the kind,' Clifford replied before Lexa could make an answer to this not very serious suggestion. 'Eight o'clock is the earliest I can be ready.'

Philippe grinned and nodded.

'Why don't you come with us, Bryden?' Suzanne asked.

He stared at the girl for a moment before replying, 'Too busy. Besides, five is an awkward number.'

'We could always take two cars,' Suzanne said quickly.

Bryden shook his head. 'I've an appointment at Evisa at midday.'

'Evisa?' echoed Suzanne. 'Then you could come up to Vizzavona afterwards. We could all meet and——'

Bryden set down his wineglass with deliberation. 'You've evidently not looked at a map of your island recently, or you'd know that the journey would be quite easy—except for the fact that the mountains are in the way, there's no road except for a very roundabout route. In any case, I expect to be occupied at Evisa all day.'

Suzanne's fair face flushed a little at this uncalled-for sarcasm. The girl turned away and began a lively conversation with Edgar.

It was after dinner when everyone was in the drawing-room and Lexa had accompanied Gabrielle in a violin sonata that the bombshell dropped into Lexa's lap. She was hardly sure that she had heard Edgar's whispered words correctly, but when he smiled, gave her a gentle tap on the shoulder and murmured, 'Think it over,' she realised that he was in earnest.

During the rest of the evening she moved around in a dream, dazed by the prospect held out before her, yet not daring to hope that she could take advantage of it. Of course she would have to consult Clifford, and if he did not agree with the arrangement, that would be the end of the idea.

She was glad when the small party broke up early, bearing in mind the next day's start for the trip to Vizzavona. In her room she could be alone to weigh up the pros and cons. All her nature swung her towards acceptance of Edgar's offer, but her sense of gratitude, of fair play and consideration for Clifford presented strong opposition.

On the outing to Vizzavona next day it was natural that whenever the foursome formed into two couples, she should be in the company of Philippe while Clifford escorted Suzanne. She was glad of this, for she was thus relieved of the temptation to unburden herself to Clifford.

Philippe was more than usually attentive, especially at lunch, which was served at a table under a canopy of tree branches outside a small village inn. Smoked sausage made of pork liver, which Philippe told her was called '*figatelli*', was followed by baked trout with almonds, then a stew with pork and tomatoes and finally chestnut flour fritters fried in olive oil, accompanied by dried figs.

11

'Always you will eat well in the country inns of Corsica,' remarked Philippe, as he poured more wine into her glass.

'Fortunately,' broke in Clifford, 'they still preserve their own local dishes instead of trying to copy the international type of food that so often you get in hotels.'

When the coffee was poured Philippe handed Lexa a small glass of liqueur. 'Try this. It's made from myrtle berries.'

She sipped carefully, noting the strong fragrance and unusual flavour. 'A wonderful drink,' she commented. 'And inexpensive to make, seeing that so many myrtle bushes grow in the *maquis*.'

'The berries are free, certainly, but they have to be collected, and that takes time and energy,' Philippe pointed out.

'So do grapes before they become wine,' she retorted. 'One can't expect the bottles to hang ready-made on the bushes.'

They all laughed, including Suzanne, who had relaxed in her chair and apparently given herself up to day-dreaming.

'You must bring Lexa to more of the inns in the mountains,' she said.

Philippe leaned towards Lexa. 'You have only to say which parts of the island you prefer and I shall be delighted to take you. And Clifford, of course,' he added belatedly, but with a slyly mischievous glance at the other man.

Clifford gave a mild grunt. 'All very well—for both of us, but we're leaving for home in three or four days.'

'Then there must be another visit to our island before long,' Philippe continued, giving Lexa a slow smile, his dark eyes gleaming. 'You must not be allowed to forget us.'

'Oh, we shan't do that,' Clifford assured him. 'We've enjoyed ourselves every minute of the time.'

Lexa remained silent, merely nodding agreement with Clifford. Her mind was busy with the possibilities that Edgar had opened out for her, but there might also be disadvantages—and one of them was named Philippe. In any case she had not yet made a final decision, so there was no need to mention the subject to Clifford. If she decided

12

against, then she would not talk about it until she and Clifford were home, and perhaps not even then. He must not be made to feel at any time that he had been responsible for her losing a tempting opportunity.

After lunch Philippe drove along a road above a valley; in the afternoon sunlight, yellow catkins dangling on the sweet chestnut trees gleamed golden against the glossy green leaves. This was contrasting country to the hillsides covered with scented *maquis* or the plunging, jagged cliffs on the west coast. One could spend half a lifetime driving or walking about this lovely island, she thought, but then abruptly shut her mind to this stretch of fancy. One should guard against the lure of scenery, yet how was it possible not to be affected by beautiful surroundings?

The last three days of the holiday went speedily, for Clifford was anxious to cram further visits to favourite places, swimming in the little coves, strenuous climbs up the hills, into these last memories of a delightful holiday.

He gave a dinner party on the last evening but one, at one of the best hotels in Ajaccio for the Franklands, inviting also Philippe and Suzanne, as well as several other young people whom he and Lexa had met. Even Bryden managed to come, and when Lexa danced with him after dinner, she was surprised by his apparent friendliness. Perhaps, she thought, he had dropped that rather distant manner because she and Clifford would soon be going home.

'So very soon you'll be all set for the job in the solicitors' office?' he queried.

'I suppose so,' she answered warily.

'Won't you find it rather humdrum after the excitement of the department store?'

For a second she met his glance, saw the baiting expression in his grey eyes, and swiftly lowered her lids. 'Selling scarves to teenagers is wildly exciting. Not many of them buy gloves, except woollen mitts, but helping older women to decide on the merits of suede or nylon or whether size six will fit their tiny hands is—frankly hilarious.'

She felt the slight intake of his breath as he checked a

laugh. 'And perhaps you'll find more gaiety in typing counsel's opinions or wills and evidence for the defence?'

The dance had come to an end. She wondered if he had an ulterior motive in probing into her future. Had Edgar told his son of his offer?

Suzanne claimed Bryden before Lexa had to find an answer to his query and now, for the first time, it occurred to Lexa that Suzanne adopted a possessive attitude towards the young Frankland. Natural, perhaps, when they were all close neighbours, but perhaps no more than a passing attraction.

On the way home Lexa happened to sit next to Bryden in one of the cars. 'Tomorrow's your last day here,' he said. 'I shall probably be out all day, so if I don't see you before you leave, I hope you have a pleasant journey home.'

'You sound as though you're rather glad to see the back of us—Clifford and me,' she replied lightly.

'Not at all. You'd be welcome to stay as long as you chose. I'm merely trying to be polite. I wouldn't like to let you both go without the usual Corsican farewell. You know what that is?'

'Not precisely.'

'Translated, one says "Goodbye till tonight or next time you pass this way. Bon voyage." All the country people still use it.'

Suzanne leaned over from the front seat. 'Perhaps Lexa won't pass this way again or come to Corsica another time?'

'I can't say,' Lexa replied. 'Depends on Clifford, of course.'

'Naturally,' agreed Bryden. 'Your future is of course bound up with his.'

Lexa made no reply, unwilling to commit herself in this casual fashion, but Suzanne sighed delicately. 'How comforting to have one's future all mapped out! To know who loves you and whom you love. I wish I knew what would happen to me in the next few years.'

'Probably all sorts of unpleasant things,' Bryden observed crisply. 'How can any of us know exactly where our actions will lead us?'

This slant on the philosophy of life was cut short by arrival at the Franklands' house, Fontenay, and in the flurry of goodnights and good wishes, Lexa was able to escape to her room.

Tomorrow was now her last chance of broaching the all-important subject to Clifford. She had not yet given any definite answer to Edgar, but the talk with Clifford must come first.

How would he take it? Clifford enjoyed argument and because of his trained mind in the legal profession was usually confident that he could overcome the opposition. Where Lexa was concerned, he was nearly always successful in convincing her that his opinion was the right one and now she was apprehensive lest her own resolve faltered and she meekly gave in. But on this occasion she must be strong.

Next morning as soon as she met Clifford after breakfast, she suggested, 'Let's walk down to the shore.'

'Well, as it's our last full day, I thought we might visit Bonifacio again. Interesting old place.'

'Perhaps we could go there later? After lunch?'

He shook his head. 'Wouldn't give us time enough.'

'Clifford, I must talk to you. It won't take long, but it's —it's rather important.'

'Oh, very well. What have you to confess? Fallen in love with Philippe?' His eyes were amused as he glanced down at her.

She laughed. 'Nothing like that.'

As they walked through the wooded path down to the shore, she remained silent. Was her decision wise? With Clifford her life might be mapped out, uncomplicated, yet an inner desire urged her to try the unknown.

'Well, fire away,' he prompted. 'Why so mysterious?'

'Wait until we're on the beach.'

He flung himself face downwards on the soft sand, resting his chin on his closed fists, and gave her a mischievous glance.

For a moment she could not find the right words.

'Such a terrible admission?' he queried.

'I'm not going back to England—not yet, anyway,' she said in a rush.

In one lithe movement he sat up and stared at her. 'Not going back—but we can't stay any longer. Or at least, I can't stay. I've all kind of engagements and commitments at home.'

'I know that, but please listen.'

'Go on. I'm listening.' His tone was grim and Lexa's courage almost vanished.

'The Franklands, Edgar and Marguerite, have asked me to stay for a while, a few months perhaps, so that I can accompany Gabrielle with her violin practice.'

Put like that, she knew it all sounded absurd. When she glanced at Clifford's face, she knew it was doubly absurd.

'You must be out of your mind! What on earth has got into you?'

She looked down at the soft hillocks of sand near her feet. 'Only that I want to do something that's congenial. Edgar thinks I can also be useful to him in copying his scores. He's composing a new symphony and several other works.'

Clifford laughed harshly. 'My dear girl, just because you once worked in the piano department of a store, you really shouldn't have idealised dreams of becoming the great composer's amanuensis. What sort of career d'you think you're going to have writing down semiquavers in three flats or tinkling out waltzes for Gabrielle's scrapings?'

She looked up sharply. 'I have some qualifications in music,' she began, but he interrupted with, 'Besides, I thought you'd already agreed to take the job in the solicitors' office, which I've arranged for you.'

'I don't know whether I'd be much use in a solicitors' office. Perhaps I'm not cut out for legal work.'

'But I've arranged it,' he protested.

'I know—and I'm truly grateful to you, Clifford, for doing this for me, but—that was before we came here— and things have changed.'

He grasped her wrist. 'What do you mean by that?

16

That you've changed?'

Lexa hesitated. Having gone so far, she knew she must take that further step and be honest with the man at her side.

'Maybe I *have* changed. Perhaps I never was the girl you thought I was.' She hardly knew what made her say those words.

'Well, well!' he muttered. 'So all this time I've been dancing to your tune! You waited until we arrived here and then sized up how the land lay. Now you spring this on me that you want to stay in Corsica on a trumped-up pretext of dabbling in Edgar's musical affairs.'

'There's no pretext about it at all,' she said angrily. 'Ask Edgar if you want the truth.'

'Undoubtedly he'll tell me the truth—that you worked on his good nature to let you stay for Gabrielle's sake.'

'That's not true!'

'Then who is the real attraction here? Philippe? Or could it be Bryden?'

'Certainly not either! Philippe likes mild flirtations with girls he has just met and forgets them in a fortnight. As for Bryden——' she paused.

'Yes? Go on. Tell me how Bryden appeals to you.'

'He doesn't,' she snapped. 'And if you'd used your eyes, you'd have seen that I simply have no appeal at all for him.'

'Then there must be some strong magnet here that I haven't understood,' Clifford said slowly, looking across the beach at the azure sea.

'Would you understand that I might want to stay here of my own accord, to do work that I know I'm fitted for. Gabrielle needs constant practice if she's to be admitted in the autumn to the Paris Conservatoire.'

'The Franklands could hire a girl here on the island just to thump out accompaniments for Gabrielle,' retorted Clifford.

'No doubt they could,' agreed Lexa swiftly. 'Perhaps they'll find me unsuitable after a week or two, send me home and—as you say—hire a local girl.'

'Then if you think that's likely to happen or could

happen, your prospects here are very shaky. You're throwing away the chance of a very successful career for the sake of a few months' idling in what's no more than a holiday job.'

'I shan't be idling, as you call it. I expect to work regular hours for Gabrielle's sake and at least earn my keep.'

'Does Edgar expect to pay you any kind of salary?'

'We haven't discussed the terms yet. I thought I should tell you about the proposition first.'

Clifford remained silent for a few moments. Then he said slowly, 'I don't know that I ought to consent at all to this mad scheme. I don't care for the idea of leaving you here with the Franklands and——'

'But the Franklands are *your* friends,' she pointed out.

'I don't know them all that well. I met Edgar a few times over legal matters, and then his wife, when the case was settled and they took me to dinner. When they invited me to stay here for a week or so, I never imagined this would happen. I'm damned sorry I brought you here, but I thought I was doing you a kindness in the matter of a holiday.'

Perhaps it was his slightly patronising tone that aroused Lexa's indignation. She would certainly not remind him that she had paid her own air fare and that staying with the Franklands had not involved any hotel expenses.

'I'm appreciative of all you've done, arranging the holiday, arranging the job for me when I go back, but even if it sounds disloyal, I find I don't want everything planned for me. I'm twenty-two and capable of looking after myself and earning a living. If the idea of helping Gabrielle doesn't turn out well, then I can always find something else.'

Clifford gave her a hard glance. 'What you mean is that you'll be content to be a drifter, blown about like a piece of thistledown. If being a musical *au pair* girl doesn't suit, you'll sell souvenirs in a boutique in Ajaccio or Capri or somewhere.'

Now she in her turn remained silent and he continued, 'I'd no idea you were like this, Lexa. No sense of loyalty or responsibility. Don't you want a settled kind of existence?'

She faced him and her eyes held the utmost seriousness.

18

'Not yet. I don't want everything cut and dried.'

He nodded and there was the hint of a sneer around his mouth. 'Then that undoubtedly applies to us. It will be a couple of years before I can think of marrying, and now I'm not sure if I'm the man for you.'

'Or that I'm the girl for you?' she hazarded. 'Look, Clifford, let's part good friends, the way we've always been. After all, we were not—engaged.'

'Just as well!' he interposed drily.

'I've never taken it for granted that you wanted to marry me.'

'I see. I was just a useful escort. Most girls like to have at least one man in tow.'

After a minute or two he rose, thrust his hands in the pockets of his shorts. 'You've wrecked our last day here, so I'll leave you to your own devices.' He marched away and disappeared up the slope through the *maquis* bushes towards the path that led to the Franklands' house.

Lexa remained and stared unseeingly at the sandy beach and the sapphire sea. Had she made a wise decision? She had been apprehensive of Clifford's reaction, but if she had turned down Edgar's offer and said nothing about it, would she have regretted declining an opportunity so unexpectedly thrust in her way?

Even now if she changed her mind and returned to England with Clifford, as arranged, matters would never be quite the same between them. It was true that she had never expected him to marry her. He had never at any time admitted that he loved her, his goodnight kisses had been no more than the salute of a companionable man friend and she had never been excited to expectant desire. When she thought about him, she had always imagined that sooner or later he would find a more attractive girl, possibly with well-to-do parents. He was ambitious in his career and marriage must be a stepping stone upwards, not a handicap imposed by an alliance with a penniless girl like Lexa.

She regretted very much that her friendship with him had been broken in this unexpected way, but she knew that if an attractive opening connected with his career had presented itself, Clifford would certainly not have let it slip for Lexa's sake.

A glance at her watch indicated that soon it would be lunchtime and Lexa climbed up the path to the house. Clifford did not appear for the meal and Marguerite remarked that he had gone to Bonifacio.

'You didn't want to accompany him?' she asked Lexa.

'No.'

After lunch she sought Edgar and told him that she had definitely decided to accept his offer.

'What does Clifford say?'

'He's not at all pleased,' replied Lexa gently. 'He had an excellent job lined up for me at home.'

'Yes, in the legal profession, I gather?'

Lexa smiled. 'Naturally. But I would like to stay here, if you want me to help Gabrielle and you think I can be useful to her.'

'Useful to us all,' Edgar assured her. 'Gabrielle needs an accompanist who will really make her work. Marguerite hasn't always the time, for she concerns herself with the housekeeping and also likes to amuse herself in many ways —cello, visits to friends, shopping, trips to Rome sometimes, or Paris. You could also be a good influence on Gabrielle, who is very young and doesn't know yet whether she really wants a musical career or a handsome young man to marry her when she is nineteen, and provide her with a château in France, a villa here on the coast and whatever else she fancies.'

Lexa smiled. 'I don't really visualise myself as an elder sister, but——'

'Oh, you'll have tact and discretion, I know. Gabrielle can be led, but not driven. Now we must sort out the details of our arrangement. I have them all ready here.' He opened the drawer of his desk and took out a couple of sheets of paper.

'Then you thought I'd accept?' Lexa queried.

'I hoped you might,' he answered, 'but even if you hadn't, there'd have been no harm in setting out the financial side of the matter. If you'd gone home, then there would have been an end of it.'

Lexa listened while Edgar briefly ran over what might be called 'her duties'. 'Not too many hours at a time, but regular sessions every day. Sometimes you may have leisure to make fair copies of my musical scrawls, but that you will be free to do whenever you choose.'

When he told her of the salary that he and Marguerite had agreed upon, she was amazed. 'Far too much,' she said, working out the amount of francs.

'Not in the least. Each month I shall pay the sum into a banking account in Ajaccio and you will be able to spend it as you like.'

'But I shall be living here—as your——'

'As our guest,' he finished for her. 'And most welcome at that.'

'I hardly know how to thank you,' she murmured.

'We'll see that we don't work you to death,' Edgar promised. 'That would upset everyone's apple-cart.'

For the rest of the day Lexa moved around in a dream-like state. The prospect for the next few months was more than she had ever hoped for. She would be able to save part of her salary and take it home in the autumn so that if she failed to find a new job immediately, she would have a balance to cushion her. She would give her Aunt Beatrice money to replace some of the furnishings in the home she shared with her, as well as send regular sums to make up for the fact that she would not be supplying some of the housekeeping money during the next few months.

Clifford did not appear for the rest of the day and came home only when Lexa was just going up to bed. He gave her a curt 'Goodnight' and went upstairs to his room.

Lexa felt as though she had received a slap in the face, but reflected that while she had had time to think over Edgar's proposition, the news had been a sudden shock to Clifford. Perhaps she should have discussed it with him earlier, instead of waiting until the last day of the holiday, but it was done now and there was no point in regretting.

It had been arranged that she and Clifford would drive to the airport at Ajaccio to catch the afternoon plane to

21

Paris, where they would change for the flight to Heathrow. Now she was uncertain whether to accompany him to Ajaccio or get the goodbyes over here in Edgar's house.

In any case, by ten o'clock next morning Clifford had not made an appearance. Sophie, the housekeeper, confirmed that she had taken his breakfast of coffee and rolls to his room earlier than usual, as he had asked, and although his suitcases were packed, there was no sign of him.

'Where can he have gone?' queried Marguerite anxiously. 'An early morning swim?'

Lexa shook her head. 'I doubt it. He doesn't usually care to swim until about midday.'

'We must send out a search party,' declared Gabrielle with more enthusiasm than anxiety. 'He may have fallen over the cliffs or——' she paused dramatically before continuing, 'or he may have walked into the sea because you are staying here, Lexa.'

'Stop talking nonsense, Gabrielle,' rebuked her mother sharply. 'Edgar must go down to the shore and the rest of us will search the garden.' Marguerite walked briskly along the terrace and towards that part of the garden. Lexa watched her, an elegant medium height well-proportioned figure with the true Parisian air about her. Even as early as this she was smartly dressed in a lemon-coloured tailored silk dress, hair style and make-up immaculate.

Lexa was rather more concerned about Clifford's non-appearance than she wanted anyone else to know. Obviously he had not dashed off earlier to the airport, for his luggage was still here.

Then as she turned a corner of the kitchen garden she saw him and ran to meet him, almost throwing herself into his arms out of sheer relief, but fortunately she managed to restrain herself in time.

She noticed immediately that he was limping badly. 'Are you hurt?' she asked.

He gave her a measured glance of distaste. 'Physically or otherwise?' he queried. After a moment he said, 'I took a tumble down by the shore—and I think I've sprained my knee.'

22

'Oh, Clifford!' she exclaimed with ready sympathy.

'Don't "Oh, Clifford" me, please,' he rebuked her. 'I daresay I can manage to get to the house without your help.'

Indoors he was immediately helped to a settee, surrounded by solicitous attention from Marguerite, Gabrielle, Sophie the housekeeper, and Edgar, while Lexa hovered in the background, unwilling to receive further brusque remarks from Clifford.

'You must stay with us and rest,' declared Marguerite warmly.

'Cancel the plane passage and we will look after you,' promised Gabrielle.

'Well, it's obvious that you can't leave today,' said Edgar, more practical than the others.

'But I must,' protested Clifford, rising from his reclining position. 'Everything's arranged. *I* have my work to think about.' The glance he cast at Lexa indicated clearly that he thought little of those who dallied on extended holidays long after the departure date had gone.

'But one day, surely——' pleaded Gabrielle.

'We must fetch the doctor,' said Marguerite decisively.

'No need for that,' objected Clifford. 'I shall be able to manage, I think—with a little help.'

Lexa was dismayed at the turn her thoughts had taken. How serious was this knee injury? Anything more than a distressing twist which would right itself in a few hours? Or was this Clifford's method of blackmailing her into accompanying him back to England?

At length he was persuaded to allow Edgar to telephone the airport at Ajaccio, cancelling today's flight and provisionally booking one seat for tomorrow.

When Clifford had been helped to a chaise-longue in the garden, a sun umbrella erected at the right angle, a table with drinks and newspapers placed at his elbow, Edgar whispered to Lexa, who had been commanded to fetch Clifford's sun-glasses, 'Does this change matters for you, Lexa? Should you go back now with Clifford and perhaps come to us later? In a week or two, perhaps?'

23

She shook her head. 'If I go home to England now, I shall never be able to come back. There will always be some claim on me to make me stay there. But thank you for asking me, Edgar.'

She sped upstairs to Clifford's room for the sun-glasses. Three suitcases stood on the floor, but when she picked up one to move it out of her way, it was obviously empty, as were the others. She opened the wardrobe and all his clothes still hung there.

But of course, she reminded herself, he had intended to pack everything when he came back from his morning walk down to the shore. Men usually rammed their possessions into suitcases in half the time that girls more carefully did their packing.

When she returned to Clifford's side, Philippe and his sister Suzanne were there, commiserating with him.

In a few moments Philippe managed to draw Lexa away to the end of the terrace, while Suzanne remained with Clifford.

His eyes were alight with pleasure. 'This is great news that I've just heard.'

'What? That Clifford has damaged his knee?' She made her voice sound indignant.

'No, no, of course not. Poor chap. No, I mean that you intend to stay here at Fontenay with the Franklands for a long time. Oh, I'm overjoyed! We shall be able to get to know each other. I'll take you to places all over the island. I'll——'

Lexa was laughing. 'Philippe, stop planning my time for me! Perhaps you haven't heard that I'm not staying just to gallivant all over Corsica, but to help Gabrielle with her practice.'

'Yes, yes, indeed. But you will not be strapped to the piano all day and every day. Edgar will surely treat you kindly?'

'I expect he will, but I shan't have a lot of free time.'

'Enough for me to take you out occasionally,' he insisted.

Then, to Lexa's surprise, Bryden approached.

Philippe turned towards him eagerly. 'I was just congratulating myself on such good news. That Lexa is staying here with your family.'

The steady glance that Bryden gave her was disconcerting. It was apparent that he did not share Philippe's enthusiasm, but since he was often away from home, it might not matter to Lexa whether he disapproved of her or not.

'I hope it'll prove a wise decision on your part,' he now said slowly to Lexa. With a muttered excuse, he walked away to the far end of the terrace and disappeared round the corner.

'Well!' exclaimed Philippe. 'He is a very dull Englishman, that one. Perhaps he has no time for girls—unless he prefers those he finds in secret places all around the island. When he goes away for several days, who would know who are his companions?'

Lexa half smiled, for her thoughts were still with Bryden's rather unwelcoming attitude. But then she pushed such trivial notions out of her mind. He was English, not a young volatile French-Corsican who might display every eagerness for her company today and tomorrow and at the end of a fortnight direct his enthusiasms towards his newest girl acquaintance.

Philippe and Suzanne stayed to lunch. 'We came,' Philippe exclaimed, 'to accompany you both to the airport, but now that Lexa is not leaving, I shall come again tomorrow, for then I can bring Lexa back here to Fontenay.'

He smiled at her over his wineglass, and she saw the query in his dark eyes, but she would not commit herself.

The rest of the day was an uncomfortable time for her. Whenever she sat with Clifford, he remained sulky or made pointed remarks to the effect that she need not feel obliged to spend time with him if she preferred some of the others in the house.

'I still think you've become attracted to Philippe,' he said after dinner when they were alone in the drawing-room. It seemed that all the rest of the Franklands had urgent business elsewhere, thus contriving to leave Clifford and Lexa together on this last night.

'Not in the least,' she replied, forcing her voice to an indifference. 'He's likeable, but not, I think, very stable in his affections.'

'Well, I suppose I must believe what you say. Of course you know that Suzanne is madly in love with Bryden.'

'No, I didn't know—although I suppose one could have guessed, perhaps.'

Clifford adopted the expression which Lexa imagined he wore in the law court when he had scored a point. 'So I think there's little chance there for you, Lexa dear. Suzanne is a determined young woman and will probably wear him down in the end.'

Lexa laughed softly. 'You seem to have mapped out Bryden's fate completely.'

He shrugged. 'I've learned to study people's characters and quite often I know which way they'll jump.'

She became silent for a few moments. Then she said, 'I'm sorry it's had to end like this, Clifford. I mean that sincerely.'

'There was nothing really to end, was there?' He gave her an amused glance. 'We were good friends, that's all. Marriage for me is still some way off and then——'

'Yes, I know, Clifford,' she broke in hurriedly. 'The girl you marry won't be like me. I'm not really the right type for you.'

He pursed his lips. 'You take a realistic view, my dear, but I think you're probably right. As a matter of fact and I'm sure you won't mind if I tell you now, but sometimes it's quite useful for a man in my position to give the *appearance* of having a steady girl-friend. It does help to keep other girls at least at a distance.'

Lexa controlled the gasp that almost escaped her. So she had been merely a convenient local girl to take about, to use to fend other girls off! She had always known of Clifford's arrogance, but regarded it as part of his ambitious plans for his life ahead. Now she knew that his conceit, his high opinion of himself and his attractions, would always have created a barrier between him and herself.

'Well, when you go home, you'll be able to invite one of

those girls at a distance to be your companion. She might even prove to be the one you're looking for.'

He grunted quietly. 'If she has patience enough to wait. I'm not ready for marriage yet. I have to put all my energies into my career. Many barristers don't marry until they're at least forty.'

'Thirteen years to go,' she murmured lightly. 'As for me, I'd be thirty-five and well past my youth.'

To her own astonishment, Lexa warmed towards Clifford, for she saw that he was at least being honest with both her and himself. If they had never come to Corsica for this holiday, they might both have gone jogging along year after year until the inevitable happened. Clifford would find another girl, suitable, of the right type, willing to join her life to his—and Lexa would be cast out with a few well-chosen words, clichés such as 'it was best for all concerned' and 'let's make a clean break'.

More important was the fact that had the opportunity to stay not arisen, she would have been unable to make the break herself, or at least it would have been more difficult.

So now it was more amicably settled between them and she was glad, for it was a weight lifted from her. When she accompanied him to the airport at Ajaccio next day, she noticed that he was scarcely limping at all. He had claimed that his knee was badly swollen, but since he was wearing dark green trousers, the fact could hardly be established.

All the Frankland family as well as Philippe and Suzanne went to wave farewell to Clifford. At the last minute when all the embraces and goodbyes were being said, Clifford held Lexa's hands for a moment. 'You're sure I can't persuade you to come back with me—even at this eleventh hour?'

She smiled gently. 'No, not even at this last minute.' She knew that his words were not intended for her, but for the others. He was putting her into the position of a head-strong girl who cared nothing for anyone else as long as she could have her own way.

When the plane took off, the little group ambled towards the exit. Philippe took Lexa's arm. 'You came in Edgar's car, but you must let me drive you back to Fontenay,' he said with unmistakable ardour.

'I can't do that,' she protested mildly. 'Edgar wouldn't like that.' She had no desire to be alone with Philippe on the long drive back.

Unexpectedly she found herself driving alone with Bryden instead. 'I'll take your car,' he told his father. 'I have a small detour to make to call on someone on the way back. So I'll take Lexa and you others can come in Philippe's car—if it won't break down,' he added with a grin.

She was ushered into the passenger seat and he was driving out of the car park before the others had sorted themselves out.

'Tell me,' he said when they were out on the main road, 'what is "Lexa" short for. Is it a nickname?'

'I was christened Alexandra, but at school it soon became shortened either to Alex or Sandra, but I preferred Lexa.'

'Why are you so anxious to stay here in Corsica?' was his next question, and she felt that no advantage would be gained if she gave devious answers.

'In the first place I was quite happy to come for a holiday. I never expected to stay here, but your father offered me this—temporary post of helping Gabrielle and I think I'd have been foolish not to have seized the opportunity.'

Too late, she knew she had made a mistake in using the word 'seized'. 'Do you often go about looking for opportunities to seize?' he asked in a deceptively innocent manner.

'Not at all. If I'd been completely settled in a congenial job at home in England, I'd have been happy to return to it.'

'And all the jobs in sight were distasteful or not to your liking?'

'You appear to think that I don't really like work,' she said warmly. 'I can assure you that I shall certainly not shirk any duties your father gives me.'

'I'm sure you won't find him a very hard taskmaster.' After a pause, during which Lexa reflected that he had deliberately whisked her away from the airport for the return journey so that he could catechise her, he returned to what she now regarded as the attack. 'And Clifford? The

28

prospect of marrying him was also not to your liking?'

'Clifford won't be able to marry for quite a few years,' she snapped.

'So you preferred not to wait too long.'

'You're putting your own—and quite wrong—construction on what I say. In any case, it's a matter between Clifford and me.'

'Of course,' he agreed with a bland smile. 'I should have known better than to mention the subject. Would you like some tea or coffee? We can stop at the next place, Propriano.'

'I thought you said you had a business call to make,' she pointed out.

'So I have. At Propriano.'

So he was stopping for his own advantage rather than being solicitous on her behalf. 'Thank you, then. I'd like some coffee.'

When the waiter set down the coffee cups, she became aware that Bryden was treating her to a prolonged stare. She felt uncomfortable under his scrutiny and looked away across the street. He had this trick of sizing up people, apparently to their disadvantage.

'If you don't mind staying here for twenty minutes or so, I'll make my business call and rejoin you,' he said when he had finished his coffee.

'I shall be safe here, no doubt. I understand that Corsican bandits are now past history.'

She met his mocking glance and saw his mouth lift in a faint smile. 'History, they say, always repeats itself, but not quite in the same manner. I'll ask Gustave, the proprietor, to keep a fatherly eye on you during my absence.'

He was gone before she could frame a suitable retort.

For the first time since she had definitely accepted Edgar's offer to stay in Corsica, a hint of doubt needled into her mind. Would Bryden accept her presence in the household as a welcome, if temporary, member? Already on a previous occasion he had thinly veiled his disapproval in contrast to Philippe's enthusiastic reaction. Today, now that Clifford had left for England, Bryden had lost no time in reinforcing his own hostility against her.

She could only hope that his business affairs on behalf of his parents would keep him away in other parts of the island for long spells. Yet she knew that each time he returned he would have a disturbing influence on her peace of mind. She had pledged herself to Edgar and Marguerite to stay until the end of September. This was now May and autumn was a long time ahead, but she was determined not to allow anyone to disrupt the harmony between her and the Frankland family. At least, she would take care not to be at fault, but were there others beside Bryden who had tolerated her as a holiday guest, but were not prepared to receive her for a more lengthy stay? Philippe was only too eager, but his sister, Suzanne? Lexa would have to test the girl's attitude at the earliest opportunity.

CHAPTER TWO

THE opportunity to explore Suzanne's attitude came to Lexa sooner than she had anticipated. By the time Bryden drove into the courtyard of his home, Fontenay, Philippe and the others had already arrived.

Philippe hurried towards Lexa while Bryden was taking his own car into one of the garages. 'Lexa! We were most worried. Why did you take so long on the journey? We thought perhaps some accident——?'

'Perhaps Bryden mistook the road and you went up into the mountains,' interposed Suzanne, 'or down to the shore to bathe.'

'Neither,' explained Lexa with a disarming smile. 'Bryden had a business call in Propriano and we stopped there for a coffee.' She had seen the frown on Suzanne's face and heard the sharp edge in the girl's voice.

'Then come now down to the beach,' invited Philippe. 'This is still your holiday and Edgar will not expect you to start thumping pianos for Gabrielle today. What about you, Suzanne?'

'One moment.' Suzanne ran towards the garage from which Bryden was emerging. Lexa watched the other girl clasp both hands around Bryden's elbow. Then he smiled and shook his head. Suzanne's downcast expression revealed that Bryden had refused whatever request she had made.

She rejoined Lexa and Philippe and made a valiant attempt to be cheerful. 'Bryden has work to do—*of course*! Accounts or something. I'll get my towel and bikini from the car and come down to the beach with you!'

There was no one else on the little sandy beach when the three arrived and Lexa could detect a certain challenge in the air.

Suzanne did not enter the water, but lay stretched out on a towel. Philippe was still swimming when Lexa came up the beach and rejoined Suzanne. When she had dried herself, Lexa followed her companion's example and stretched herself out on a dry towel, but now Suzanne sat up suddenly.

'What is your impression of Bryden?' she asked.

Straight to the point, Lexa reflected. 'Well, I don't know him. I've met him only three or four times.'

Suzanne smiled encouragingly. 'Oh, but you must have a first impression of any man. As for me, that is what counts. If I like a person straightaway, then it is lasting. If I do not —then that person is never attractive to me.'

'And what was *your* first impression of Bryden?' Lexa saw no reason against landing the other girl with such a loaded question.

Suzanne clasped her hands dramatically and raised her glance towards the cloudless blue sky. 'Oh, he was—he was everything I had dreamt of that a man should be! I fell in love with him in that first instant.'

'Have you known him a long time?'

'Over a year. He came in the spring of last year. I remember the date. It was the nineteenth of April.'

'And your first impressions have been confirmed?' Lexa queried.

'Yes, indeed. A hundredfold.'

Lexa was silent for a minute or so. She was reluctant to ask if Bryden reciprocated Suzanne's ecstatic feelings. That would be a delicate and personal question, but Lexa felt a compelling urge to know the answer. Why should it matter if Bryden and Suzanne made a match when by the autumn she, Lexa, would be far away in England?

Yet the question came tumbling out, almost of its own accord. 'And Bryden? Does he?—are his feelings for you the same?'

'But of course!' Suzanne turned a surprised glance towards Lexa. 'He has eyes for no one but me. But there are difficulties. There are always difficulties when two people love each other, so he cannot make his attitude very plain.'

'And the difficulties?' prompted Lexa.

'Well, you will understand that Philippe and I are not well off. My father makes a little money buying and selling land, sometimes other things—crops from the country parts. But my *dot* will be small, whoever I marry.'

'But surely that would not matter where Bryden is concerned? The Frankland family seem fairly comfortable, financially.'

Suzanne nodded. 'That is so, I believe. But my father is true Corsican and it would hurt his pride if I married a foreigner and had no appropriate dowry to take with me.'

Lexa first blinked, then laughed softly. 'But surely this is out of date. Who would bother nowadays?'

Suzanne's face became grave. 'Corsicans bother about such matters. It would be quite different if I were to marry a local Corsican. My father would arrange in other ways to the satisfaction of the man's family. In fact, there is already someone whom my father would very much like me to marry.'

'Oh?' Lexa's interest was aroused. 'So Bryden has a rival?'

'Certainly not!' Suzanne sounded cross. 'There will never be a rival to Bryden. I do not like this other man. He is too old for me. He is nearly forty—well, he is thirty-two——'

Lexa laughed at that. 'At your age, there's little difference between thirty-two and forty?'

'He seems old,' Suzanne shrugged. 'But I do not love him. How could I love anyone when my heart is quite filled with Bryden?'

Lexa was well aware of the significance of this conversation. As a holiday visitor, she had presented no problem to Suzanne, but now, as a temporary resident of four or five months ahead, Lexa was being warned most decisively, 'Hands off Byyden!'

Suzanne's next words reinforced this view. 'Of course, you know how it is yourself. No doubt Clifford occupies your thoughts all the time as Bryden does mine.'

It was on the tip of Lexa's tongue to establish the fact that Clifford certainly had no monopoly of her thoughts, that only the ties of friendship existed between her and him, but while she hesitated, Suzanne continued, 'I'm surprised that you could bear to be separated for so long all during the summer. Surely you and Clifford would enjoy yourselves going out, amusing yourselves in the sunshine. But perhaps you do not have much sunshine in England. Is it always foggy?'

Lexa laughed. 'That old legend dies hard. We do occasionally have a little fog, but we're not exactly shrouded in it all the year. The summer is not so hot as in Corsica, but often pleasant for long stretches.'

'You have made plans for your marriage?' queried Suzanne with a sharp, oblique glance at the other.

Lexa shook her head. 'You must understand that Clifford's career is very important to him and——'

But Philippe was standing in front of them now, reaching for his towel, and Lexa was grateful for being spared the necessity to end her sentence.

When the trio returned to the Franklands' house, Lexa studied afresh the place that would be her home for a few months. Edgar had told her that the older part of Fontenay was originally a farmhouse, four storeys tall and on rising ground. Then additions had been made, a room or two here, an extra bit there, until the long wing on one side

33

had been planned and built by Edgar himself, so that the structure was now L-shaped with the courtyard in front.

The long wing now included the dining-room and the spacious drawing-room with its grand piano. One might almost call it a salon, for there was accommodation for at least thirty people. Edgar had his own study on the upper floor and at the end of the block was a small room set aside for practice.

Philippe and Suzanne did not stay for dinner tonight and since Bryden did not appear, Lexa guessed that Suzanne had been aware of his absence and therefore had no urgent reason for staying.

'I think we'll give you and Gabrielle two or three days' grace,' Edgar decided when Lexa asked him next morning what routine she was to adopt for the practice sessions.

'In fact I think we might all go out this afternoon and idle a little time. We could go to Bonifacio, perhaps. How about you, Marguerite? Would that suit you?'

'Perfectly,' she answered. 'If you like we'll take lunch early.'

'I'll go down for a swim, then,' decided Lexa. 'I'll be back punctually at whatever time you say for lunch.'

'Twelve o'clock,' Marguerite told her with a smile.

In one way, Lexa was glad of the chance to isolate herself for an hour or two down on this delightful crescent of sand. For the last three weeks she had been constantly in the company of either Clifford or the Franklands or Philippe.

She took off her shoes and padded about on the soft sand, then down by the water's edge where a clear and glittering sea caressed the shore. A short time later, clad in an apricot-coloured bikini, she ran into the gentle waves and swam towards the horizon. After a moderate distance she turned and headed for the shore, then rolled over and lazily flung up her arms in back-stroke until she grounded in the shallows. She sat for a few moments, hugging her knees, gazing up at the arch of blue sky, then at the aquamarine sea, joyous because she was here in this lovely island and a period of interesting living stretched out before her.

Suddenly she had the notion that someone was watching her. She turned and began to wade out of the water. Bryden was lying beside her towel and beach bag as though he were a sheep dog on guard.

She wrapped herself in the towel he handed up to her, then sat down and vigorously rubbed her hair. He had not spoken, not even a civil greeting or 'Good morning', and she hunted about in her mind for words to say that would not sound too fatuous. Finally she thought that remarks about the scenery might not be too dangerously personal.

'Even so near the sea, you can still smell the scented *maquis* bushes.'

'Napoleon knew that, too,' he replied. 'When he was on St Helena he thought about his birthplace, and you probably know what he wrote—"By the fragrance of its soil alone, I would know it with my eyes closed." Have you visited his house in Ajaccio where he was born?'

'Yes, but I understood that the interior had been reconstructed since he was a child there.'

'To some extent, yes. Some of the contents were looted when he and his family were driven out of Corsica, but much of the original furniture has been restored.'

'I must try to go again. You can't take in the atmosphere on a rushed visit. Houses need your leisure to appreciate them.'

He raised himself on one elbow and watched while she brushed the tangles out of her shoulder-length bronze colour hair.

His scrutiny unsettled her, as always, and in one way she wished he had not come down to the beach this morning. In another and more disturbing direction, she was glad of his company, even though she was aware that half the time he was baiting her or that his remarks often had an underlying rudeness.

'I imagined that you had so much work to do that you couldn't spare time for idling on beaches,' she said, slyly advancing into his territory.

'This happens to be my favourite beach and, believe it or not, I really do some of my work down here, as well as on other beaches.'

'Pleasant work!' she jeered.

He sat up suddenly. 'I have to turn myself into a guinea-pig, imagine I'm a tourist here, laze in places where they might want to laze, test the winds and so on.'

'And then I suppose you decide that the beautiful deserted beach is an ideal spot to set up clusters of bunga-lows or an up-ended matchbox of an hotel?'

He smiled. 'You've probably seen only those groups of huts or holiday villages and so on that have been run up too quickly. Naturally, Corsica needs tourists, but not at the expense of wrecking the island and destroying the very qualities it has—breathtaking scenery, quiet, sheltered beaches. All it needs is discreetly-sited hotels or villas with adequate plumbing.'

Lexa nodded. 'Yes, the plumbing. Is water a problem here? There seem to be plenty of rivers.'

'Water is always a problem in Mediterranean countries. Corsica is well supplied with excellent streams straight from the mountains, but you never know when a shepherd may decide to divert a main stream for his own purposes, or perhaps a landowner dams the river at a critical point, so that his own property is well irrigated.'

'So you'll build your discreetly-sited holiday places? If the water supply is correct?'

He shook his head. 'Not on any grand scale. We haven't the capital, my father and I. You must understand that he hasn't much in the way of resources. He has a few invest-ments here and there, but the pair of them, he and Marguerite, have no head for financial matters at all. Any schoolboy could rook them.'

'I suppose you mean that because they are musicians they're not capable of understanding money?'

'Just can't be bothered, more likely. Money comes in irregularly, fees of one sort and another, and they both be-lieve they have unlimited spending power. Marguerite sails off to Paris for new clothes for herself and Gabrielle, al-though she's not altogether dependent on my father. She has a small annuity left by her husband, but she thinks it's made of elastic.'

'Then it's fortunate that they have you to look after them,' she murmured. She did not mean the words sarcastically, but she felt rather than saw his quick turn of the head towards her.

'They need protection.'

'From whom? People like me, who take advantage of your father's generosity?' What possessed her to fling the angry words at him? Yet during the last few minutes she had received the strongest impression that Bryden was warning her not to make too many demands on his father and Marguerite. He was not exactly accusing her of cosily feathering her nest, but he was making it clear that her services were an additional expense to the Frankland household.

'You seem over-ready to assume that general remarks are directed at you as accusations. I didn't mean that you were a menace.'

'Thank you,' she muttered, ashamed of her outburst. It was evident that in any battle of words with Bryden she would be the ultimate loser. Clifford had always been able to twist her arguments to his own advantage, but Bryden would be an even more formidable opponent. She must learn to tread more warily in future.

She relaxed at full length and closed her eyes. Perhaps if she indicated that she wanted to continue here on the beach sunning herself, Bryden would leave her in peace. Was that what she wanted? Certainly, she told herself fiercely. The less she had to do with Bryden Frankland, the better. In fact, she pitied Suzanne who had fallen in love with him. But perhaps he was more tender and less hostile to a neighbouring French-Corsican girl than to the English intruder who had thrust herself into the family circle.

After a short while he asked, 'Are you coming back to lunch?'

'Yes, of course. Marguerite said twelve o'clock.' She pulled on brown trousers and an apricot shirt, collected her few belongings and rolled up her towel. 'I seem to have lost my powder compact.' She knelt down in the soft sand

and searched around.

'This looks like it.' He held out the gilt compact and as she took it he grasped her wrists to help her to her feet. She was conscious of a sharp leap in her pulses and was annoyed at her reaction.

In bare feet she shuffled through the soft silvery sand, but at the edge of the path through the *maquis* she stopped to put on her sandals. Afterwards she regretted that she had not put them on earlier when she was still sitting down on the beach, for now when she rocked slightly off balance, Bryden put out a hand to steady her and his touch on her shoulder was disturbing enough to bring the hot colour to her cheeks. She bent down to adjust the fastenings, so that she could hide her face from his sharp gaze.

After lunch when Lexa was dressed and ready for the drive to Bonifacio, she was surprised to find that Bryden was to accompany his father and stepmother.

'Bryden can drive,' directed Edgar. 'He's better at it than I am. These twisty roads in the mountains make it hard going.'

Gabrielle had apparently gone off into Ajaccio, so there were only the four and when Marguerite and Edgar sat in the back, only the passenger seat next to Bryden remained.

She had visited Bonifacio twice before and knew that Bryden had to drive almost into Sartène, the nearest town, before he could reach the main road that bore south to the coast.

'I suppose one day there'll be a new road cut through?' she asked. 'Isn't there even a narrow road or a track?'

'Only for those who like scrambling through the *maquis*,' Bryden answered with a grin. 'This part of the island was very deserted until comparatively recently. Malaria always drives people away from the coast up into the hills.'

'But surely malaria has been wiped out now.'

'Yes, but only effectively in the last thirty years. That's not long in the history of an old island like Corsica.'

He drove for several miles downhill until the mountains came into view, bare stony walls streaked with vertical crevasses. Near the coast, she recognised the Lion de

Roccapina, a rock formation on the edge of the shore.

'It really does look like a crouching lion,' she murmured.

The road now swung away from the coast and there were no villages, no fishing ports, even though long claws of rock stretched far out into the sea and made natural inlets or tiny harbours.

Eventually Bryden drove through a cutting between huge limestone cliffs and then to Bonifacio harbour where boats rode at anchor and tall old houses overlooked a wide quay.

'Now what's the programme?' asked Bryden as the party alighted from the car.

'First we'll have coffee,' decided Marguerite. She turned towards Lexa. 'Have you been in the sea grottoes?'

'No.'

'Then Bryden must take you,' declared Edgar. 'The town looks impossible when viewed from a small boat.'

It was arranged that Edgar and Marguerite would stroll around the harbour in the meantime and after Lexa's boat trip all four would climb to the upper city.

Bryden had gone off to find a boatman and came back in a few minutes. 'When you're ready, Lexa.' She finished her coffee and rose obediently.

From the small boat, as Edgar had said, the town seemed impossibly perched. Ancient fortresses and yellowish houses clung to the edge of precipices where the sea had worn the soft rock into innumerable uneven steps and sea birds occupied the ledges. 'So precarious,' she murmured. 'It's a miracle the buildings don't fall straight down into the sea.'

When the boat entered the Dragon's Cave, she exclaimed with excited delight. A sheet of vivid turquoise water at the entrance led to an inner hall of immense rocks and now the water became a mosaic of fantastic colour, with the reflected light and the underwater rocks encrusted with seaweeds shimmering in jewel colours, gold, emerald, sapphire and amethyst. She dabbled her hand in the water and it seemed to hold a glittering cluster of gems.

'The loveliest sight I've ever seen,' she murmured softly, warming towards Bryden with gratitude for conducting her today.

The boatman shouted a warning to lie flat in the boat as he manoeuvred his craft out of the mouth of the cave.

When they landed at the quay, Edgar and Marguerite were waiting at the café set in the angle of two buildings where a single palm tree shaded half a dozen tables.

'You had not been in the sea caves before?' queried Marguerite as Lexa sat down.

'No. It was a marvellous sight.'

'Perhaps we didn't tell Clifford about them,' put in Edgar.

Lexa remembered that on the previous occasion, Clifford had dismissed the idea of entering the caves. 'Overrated, probably,' he had said, 'and bound to be smelly.'

When, later, she climbed with the other three up the broad cobbled ramp leading to the upper city, she remembered again that previous visit with Clifford. Somewhere along the way he had apparently dropped his sun-glasses and then spent a ridiculous amount of time and energy searching for them. When she had suggested buying a new pair at any local shop, he had objected that they were specially suited to his eyesight and really indispensable. So there had not really been time to reach the main part of the old medieval city and explore its ancient streets.

Today, Marguerite who was wearing sensible flat-heeled shoes instead of her usually elegant footwear, made only the mildest complaint. 'This pathway was made for horsemen, not people with feet.'

Lexa agreed. Even in strong sandals, the cobbled surface was not easy.

The ancient drawbridge into the walled city was still intact with iron-studded door and the chains and wheels used in its operation.

'It's like stepping back into the past,' Lexa murmured as they went through. 'You can imagine horsemen clattering over the drawbridge, a confusion of trumpets and fanfares and flying pennants.'

Bryden gave her a glance which she could not interpret. Approval for her sense of atmosphere? Or ridicule for her fanciful notions?

'You should write a piece of music about Bonifacio,' Bryden said to his father. 'All stirring trumpets and fanfares, as Lexa says.'

So he was really ridiculing her, she thought.

Edgar was laughing. 'Really, if I tried to write a piece about every scene I've come across that's exciting or historical or poetically beautiful, I'd never have time for anything else.'

'If Lexa were a composer, I'm sure she'd be inspired to write a fantasia or overture or whatever is the right term.' Bryden again gave her that quizzical glance.

'I have to be content to play the works of other people, although I did once try my hand at an original waltz—I was eight years old at the time, but certainly no embryo Strauss.'

They ambled along through the network of narrow streets, stopping to gaze at the medieval houses looming above or the churches either crumbling away or turned into museums.

When they came to the two Gothic churches which Bryden told them had been built by the Genoese, he said to Lexa, 'You should have been here for Easter. They have a colourful procession on Good Friday. Not the usual penitential affair which you can see elsewhere, but more like a festival. The crowds that follow the wooden statues carry lighted tapers with painted shades.'

'We all came specially to see it,' put in Marguerite. 'Almost every minute someone's taper catches the shade alight and then everyone is laughing and teasing while they put out the flames and light another taper.'

By now they had reached the tip of the peninsula to see the ruins of an old monastery. From here the coast of Sardinia could be seen across the strait, as well as a long strip of Corsica's own coast away to the west.

Marguerite found a comfortable place to sit on an old broken wall. 'We can watch the sunset, but from a perch to rest our feet.'

The setting sun glittered the water with a dazzling golden

light and the sky changed from blue to crimson and mauve with streaks of yellow and fiery rose. When the sun disappeared the sea became a cool violet although the rocks along the coast still glowed with colour.

Involuntarily, Lexa shivered.

'You are cold?' asked Marguerite.

'Only for the moment. When the sun goes down, you feel the temperature drop sharply.'

'Right,' said Edgar. 'We'll go smartly down to the harbour and find some food. That is, *chérie*,' he added to his wife, 'if you can totter as far.'

'To walk is better than to ride a bicycle down that stony street,' she answered with a smile.

Lexa was surprised when Bryden took her hand to guide her down the cobbled ramp. On the way up she had studiously avoided being too near him in case she stumbled and he had felt obliged to assist her.

His touch on her wrist was warm and comforting and even something more—a definite quickening of the blood. Yet she inwardly laughed at these absurd fantasies. She reminded herself that it was only yesterday that Clifford had gone home and here she was, one single day spent in the company of Bryden and she was analysing her emotions.

She was glad when they arrived down at quayside level and entered a small fish restaurant.

'You like fish?' inquired Bryden when they were seated at a table.

'Of course.'

'Good. This place serves nothing else.'

'Lexa has had all kinds of fish in our house,' remarked Edgar.

'Some I've never heard of, but all delicious,' agreed Lexa.

Bryden scanned the menu. 'Then we must search for one that might surprise you, especially if you saw it raw, on the slab in the market.'

'Bryden, you must not upset Lexa's appetite,' admonished Marguerite. 'One is not always delighted to imagine the food before it is cooked.'

When the dish came, she found it was *mostelle*, served

42

with chipped almonds and unusual herbs.

When they left the restaurant and strolled along the quayside towards the car park, Lexa watched the reflected lights dancing and glistening in the dark water. Today had been full of happiness, one to be remembered with the satisfaction that perhaps Bryden was not antagonistic towards her after all. It would have been ridiculous to imagine that he would fall over himself to entertain every passing visitor who stayed a week or two with his family.

Yet, all the same, Lexa wondered how strong was his relationship with Suzanne. Was he as much in love with her as obviously Suzanne was with him?

On the drive home, Lexa sat with Marguerite in the back of the car and the girl considered this a happy arrangement for she and her hostess could comfortably doze if they wanted to. Lexa was tired after the long day's sightseeing and had no wish to be stimulated by Bryden's nearness at the wheel.

Philippe was an early caller next morning. 'You have disappointed me,' were almost his first words after greeting Lexa on the terrace at Fontenay. 'I'd planned to take you out somewhere, but no, you had already gone with Bryden to Bonifacio.'

'Edgar and Marguerite also came,' she reminded him.

Philippe shrugged, then smiled. 'And they would prevent him taking you off somewhere alone?'

'But we stayed together all the time, the four of us,' she told him, then remembered the boat trip in the Dragon's Cave, but she saw no reason to disclose that fact to Philippe. It was already a precious memory to be cherished.

'Then where can we go today? Where would suit you?'

Lexa decided that she must not yield to this importunate young man every time he offered to take her on some excursion around the island. 'My time is already mapped out for today and tomorrow, Philippe. After that, Gabrielle and I start our daily routine, which you know about.'

He frowned heavily. 'Yes, you've taken on a heavy task. Seven days a week. No days off. I would never have believed that Monsieur Frankland could be such a hard man, to make you slave like that.'

'Life is full of surprises,' she commented lightly.

His dark eyes gleamed at her, first with approval, then clouded as he allowed his shoulders to droop in sorrow. 'Perhaps I shall soon be sorry that Clifford did not take you home with him. I can see that in the future I shall have much pain.'

She knew better than to take his remarks seriously, for she realised that most of his conversation was nothing but the small change of everyday acquaintanceship. When he had finally left with many grumbles and threats that he would call every day until she consented to go for a car ride with him, she went to her room. She had to write a long explanatory letter to her Aunt Beatrice. She had already given Clifford a short letter outlining the situation and he had promised to post it as soon as he arrived in England.

'I don't think I can call on your aunt,' he had said, 'or I might find myself saying more than I should. It's up to you, Lexa, to explain your reasons and whatever plans you have for the next few months.'

Now she sat down and wrote fully, describing the Frankland family, the house, the terms on which she would be employed.

'. . . Mr Frankland is being very generous and I shall be able to send you money from time to time to help with the housekeeping bills. I do hope you won't feel that I've let you down, after all the kindness you've shown me, but this seemed an opportunity not to be missed. When I return at the end of the summer, I'll set about finding a new job—but it won't be in a solicitor's office! Clifford is naturally vexed that I haven't accepted that offer, but I think he has more important matters to occupy him and he'll soon forget . . .'

When Lexa closed the letter she realised that apart from mentioning that Edgar had a son who spent little time at home, she had not even indicated Bryden's name, although she had written of Philippe and his sister Suzanne who were near neighbours. Lexa glanced thoughtfully out of the window in front of her. Better not to have mentioned Bryden. If Clifford did happen to meet Aunt Beatrice, which was unlikely, there would be no basis for speculation as to any ulterior motives on Lexa's part.

Bryden had apparently gone off on business journeys to Bastia and the north of the island. Lexa was relieved to have a few days without his disturbing presence in the house. No doubt she would become accustomed in time to his unsettling effect on her.

But her tranquillity was soon shattered. The next afternoon Suzanne called, driving Philippe's ramshackle old car.

'Marguerite and Gabrielle are not at home,' Lexa told her when Sophie, the housekeeper, announced Suzanne.

Suzanne smiled charmingly, but her dark eyes did not reflect any kind of pleasure.

'Dear Lexa, it was you I came to see,' she said, in a dove-like voice. 'We must talk, you and I. Is there somewhere for us to be alone?'

Lexa was now on her guard. Already she knew the subject of Suzanne's talk. 'Of course,' she agreed. 'I will ask Sophie or one of the maids to bring us tea on the terrace. Or would you prefer coffee?'

Suzanne's young face clouded slightly. 'Not here—at Fontenay. Let's go down to the shore.'

Lexa realised that Suzanne was prepared for a stormy outburst, but could not give adequate vent to her feelings if she were accepting hospitality at the house.

The two girls walked down through the woodland path. Lexa made conversational remarks about the good weather, the vista of sea and sky ahead, anything that was not controversial, but Suzanne muttered only monosyllables in reply. As soon as she had reached the beach, Suzanne flung herself on the sand and immediately attacked.

'You went to Bonifacio yesterday!' she accused.

Lexa said mildly, 'Yes.'

'With Bryden.'

'With Bryden and his father and Marguerite,' Lexa corrected. 'It was a family party.'

45

'But Bryden took you into the caves—and you were alone.'

'Yes, except for the boatman.'

Suzanne waved away in disgust such insignificant creatures as mere boatmen. 'How many times have I asked Bryden to take me into those caves!'

'But you've lived here all your life. Surely you've visited Bonifacio and the caves many times.'

'Not with Bryden,' snapped Suzanne. Obviously no other companion counted.

There was a pause. Lexa was most unwilling to quarrel with the girl, however much she was provoked. It would be a fine start to her term of employment if she caused dissension between the Franklands and Suzanne's family.

'There's no need for you to be upset because of yesterday,' she now said gently to Suzanne.

But that soothing remark proved inflammable. 'No need!' echoed Suzanne furiously. 'Before one week is gone, you will steal Bryden from me!'

'Listen, Suzanne. I've no intention of stealing anyone, and as for Bryden, do you really think one girl can steal him from another? He wouldn't be worth much if he were so easily grabbed.'

'Then next time you must refuse to go out with him.'

'I was surprised yesterday that he came with us. Actually, Edgar wanted Bryden to drive, so I suppose as he had time to spare, he agreed.'

'Time to spare to look into your beautiful eyes!' jeered Suzanne.

'I don't even remember his doing that,' retorted Lexa, beginning to be angry herself. 'If the occasion arises and he happens to be included in some excursion or other, I shall go with the rest. Or do you want me to ask your permission?'

Suzanne raised a tearful face. 'If you asked, I would not give you such freedom.'

'But, Suzanne, be sensible. I live in the house—for the time being, anyway. I can't refuse when arrangements are made.'

'And I wish that I, too, could live in the house,' the other mumbled.

'Perhaps it might do you good if you tried that for a week or two,' said Lexa impatiently. 'You'd soon find out that men dislike girls tripping about after them like little dogs. Grow up, Suzanne, and behave like a woman, not a child whose favourite toy has been put out of reach. Bryden might like you a lot better if you didn't make it so obvious that you adored him.'

Suzanne stopped in mid-sob to glare at Lexa. 'So that is your plan? You will play with him like a cat and a mouse until you make him come to you on his knees begging for your kisses.'

Lexa laughed. 'Can you imagine Bryden crawling about on his knees begging for anything? I've no plan where Bryden is concerned. You can rest assured of that.' A question needled itself at that moment into Lexa's mind. If such a plan occurred to her, would she put it into action? The situation, of course, would never arise. She had no intention of allowing herself to fall under his spell, or be reduced to the tearful, spineless state Suzanne now presented. While it was true that Bryden affected her so disquietingly in a manner she had not before experienced with other men—Clifford, certainly not Philippe—these emotions were of no account. They were merely the result of her uncertainty about his attitude, hostile, friendly or indifferent.

Suzanne had dried her eyes and was calmer now. Then she said, 'You have given me advice of what I must not do. Now it is my turn. You should be kinder to my brother. He is head over heels in love with you.'

Lexa smiled slowly. 'I think not. He may fancy he has fallen in love with me, but as soon as he meets the next girl, he'll soon forget about me.'

Suzanne gave her companion a prolonged, assessing stare. 'I think you're a very hard girl,' she said. 'Poor Philippe is unhappy because of you. Then there is Clifford —you can bear to be separated from him for many months.

But perhaps you will return then to England and marry him?'

'Possibly,' returned Lexa thoughtlessly, her mind occupied with easing Suzanne's anxieties. She was unaware of how much distress that simple admission might cause in the future.

'Come on, Suzanne,' she said, rising, and dusting the sand from her dress. 'Let's go back to the house and we'll have tea and some of Sophie's chocolate cakes that you like so much.'

Suzanne mustered a watery smile. 'You think tea and cakes will comfort me. Perhaps you hope that I shall grow fat and then Bryden——'

'Hush, Suzanne. Take your mind off the man, just for half an hour, please.'

When an hour later Lexa waved goodbye to Suzanne as the latter drove her brother's old car out of the courtyard, Lexa remained thoughtful. If Bryden loved Suzanne, although he gave little evidence of this, then Lexa must step warily and be careful not to disrupt the harmony of two people in love with each other.

CHAPTER THREE

AFTER dinner that evening, Lexa told Marguerite of Suzanne's call in the afternoon, but said nothing about the quarrel, if it could be called that.

'Suzanne invited me to spend part of the day at her home tomorrow. Would that be convenient?'

Marguerite smiled. 'Of course. Who will drive you? Or do you want to take our car?'

'Suzanne promised to come after lunch and she said she would drive me back again.'

'Unless Philippe seizes the opportunity to bring you home,' interposed Gabrielle, who had just come into the room.

Lexa nodded. 'Perhaps I shall have to learn to drive and be independent. My aunt wasn't able to afford a car and Clifford would never let me handle his.'

'I will teach you,' promised Gabrielle.

Edgar hooted with derisive laughter. 'My dear Lexa, don't accept that offer if you value your limbs. Gabrielle will have you tackling a wall or sailing over the cliff, since she doesn't know the brakes from the accelerator!'

'Not true. A libel!' she shot at him, laughing.

'Slander!' he corrected her. Lexa noted the warm, affectionate relationship that existed between the silver-haired man and his stepdaughter. Perhaps this accord was also reflected in Marguerite's attitude to Bryden, her stepson, for these two often found common ground for laughter.

Suzanne appeared in the best of moods when she arrived next day soon after lunch. She was wearing a rose-pink dress that enhanced her unusual colouring of fair hair and dark brown eyes.

Although Lexa knew that Philippe and Suzanne lived not far away, she did not know in which direction. Now Suzanne drove almost into the small town of Sartène, then took a rough track leading towards the mountains. She swung the car around bends at terrifying speed and once Lexa was forced to murmur, 'Not so fast, please, Suzanne!'

'It is not possible to slow down,' replied the other, 'or the car will not take the sharp curves, but we shall soon be at my home.'

It was only a few more minutes before the car clattered to a halt in front of an old stone house set in a wild, tangled garden.

Before starting out, Suzanne had assured Lexa that Philippe might not be at home. Or at least she had taken the opposite view and said that Philippe would be sorry to have missed Lexa's visit to his home. All the same, Lexa was not too sure that he would be absent.

Suzanne was already conducting her companion through a wide doorway where the woodwork had paled to a silver-grey and only fragments of the original paint remained.

The hall was stone-flagged and Suzanne led the way into

a fairly large, but dark room. Lexa had a vague impression of a table covered with a wine-red cloth, a couch with some bright satin cushions, half a dozen chairs of assorted design.

'Wait here and I'll tell Blanche to bring some coffee.' Suzanne disappeared through another door which apparently led to the kitchen.

The house was not only shabby, as Lexa had been told, but it seemed to be neglected and uncared-for. One of the windows had a broken pane, which had been patched with a rough piece of glass; the curtains hung in threadbare folds, their original colours now dimmed into nondescript browns and greys.

Lexa had never asked what sort of work Philippe did, if any, as she had not considered it her business to know, but now that she was viewing his home, she considered that whatever the state of his finances he certainly did not bother about simple domestic repairs. Anyone, however ham-fisted, could put a couple of screws into the hinge of one of the shutters as it hung lopsidedly against the wall.

When Suzanne returned she was followed by a plump, middle-aged woman with dark features and a thin-lipped mouth.

'This is Blanche, our housekeeper,' Suzanne said, as the woman set down the tray of coffee and small cakes on a nearby table.

When Blanche had gone, Suzanne poured the coffee. 'Now you can see that we are indeed poor, as I told you. We have none of the luxury of Bryden's family, but we can live.'

'Then Philippe does not—er—contribute?' Lexa asked as delicately as she could.

Suzanne laughed. 'Oh, sometimes he earns money—one way or another—but he spends it faster than he gets it. My father, too, has problems. He has several small businesses in various villages, but when new hotels open he loses his trade.'

'But I should have thought the opposite would happen,' Lexa suggested. 'Surely the tourists need your father's shops more than before. What does he sell?'

'Many things—wine, groceries, vegetables, fruit. But the hotel companies open their own new shops and then the visitors don't come any more to Gregorio Moriani. Also, my father has three or four small inns—the kind that take perhaps six or eight people for a night or two. But the tourists want baths and much hot water, so they go to the new places.'

'Yes, I can see the difficulties for you and your father,' murmured Lexa.

Suzanne sighed. 'And Bryden. It is plain why my father does not like him. He blames Bryden for his misfortunes.'

'Why? Bryden is not all that prominent in the hotel industry, is he?'

'No, not in the big towns like Ajaccio or even Propriano, but he is eager to improve accommodation in the small mountain villages. He is having some small villas built in several places—and always where my father is established.'

Lexa remained silent for a few moments. Then she asked, 'Your father knows that you love Bryden—and would like to marry him?'

Suzanne nodded. 'But he will never give his consent. He said he would rather see me dead than married to the man who is doing his best to ruin the Morianis.'

'Yes, you have formidable difficulties.'

'But it is tiresome to discuss business affairs. Let's talk about clothes. That outfit you're wearing is charming.'

Lexa glanced down at the pale lime-green two piece, trimmed with white at the neck and cuffs.

'Did you buy it here?' pursued Suzanne.

'No, I brought it with me, but I shall soon have to think about buying a couple more dresses. I brought only enough for a holida; 'ut now that I'm——'

Suzanne smiled genially. 'Now that you're here for a few months, you must have new dresses to catch the eye.'

'Where would you suggest are the best places?' queried Lexa. 'I can't afford really high prices.'

The other girl shrugged. 'I would hardly know. I have to make most of mine. This one'—she indicated her own rose-pink dress—'made from two metres bought in the market

51

place in Ajaccio.'

'Then you're very clever, Suzanne. You've a French-woman's sense of style.' Lexa meant the compliment sincerely, but Suzanne turned away sharply to collect the coffee cups.

'You must meet my father,' Suzanne said after a few moments. 'He's probably outside somewhere.'

Lexa followed Suzanne along a passage and through a small door that led to the back of the house. Across the yard were several outhouses in various states of disrepair, the roofs sagging, one which had collapsed altogether.

Alongside a pile of tree branches a man swung an axe to chop the logs into smaller pieces. He straightened up as Suzanne and Lexa approached.

'You must meet my friend Lexa, who is staying with the Franklands.' Suzanne spoke to her father in French.

Lexa was convinced that she had never met a man who resembled the conventional appearance of a Corsican bandit more than Monsieur Moriani. As he took off his ancient straw sun hat and scrutinised her, Lexa noted the tanned, lined face, slightly hooked nose, bristling eyebrows surmounting dark lively eyes. The luxuriant twirl of his moustache added almost a caricature touch. He wore an open-necked shirt, mud-stained breeches and boots and his hand resting on the axe was the colour of mahogany.

He gave her the merest bow of acknowledgment and did not extend his hand towards her, although Lexa guessed that he might consider his hands too dirty to proffer. All the same, she sensed the hostility in his manner, especially when he growled, 'That family!'

Suzanne laughed. 'Lexa can't help it if you don't like some people.' Then she added a few words that Lexa could not understand, probably in Corsican dialect, she supposed.

'Now you see,' Suzanne said to Lexa as they moved away across the cluttered yard, 'we have no garden or swimming pool. Nothing that is elegant, such as Bryden's home. We are not smart. And the reason'—Suzanne shrugged—'we never have any money.'

Lexa murmured a non-committal 'Mm,' but inwardly she

was thinking that between the three of them, the Morianis could have made a more comfortable habitation for themselves. Gregorio Moriani might not care if his surroundings were rough-and-ready, but surely Philippe could have spared time and energy to tidy up the place.

Lexa had not intended to stay to dinner, but finally yielded to Suzanne's entreaties. 'It is so rare that we have a guest here, unless it is some business friend of my father's, and then all they do is talk until the early hours and drink much wine.'

It was easy enough to imagine the girl's unexciting life and Lexa could sympathise with Suzanne's eagerness to get away from it through the escape route of marriage.

'Has it never occurred to you, Suzanne, to take up some kind of work?'

Lexa's innocently-intended question seemed to shock the other girl into appalled amazement, eyebrows raised to absurd levels. 'Work?' echoed Suzanne, as though the word indicated some completely foreign activity with which she would hope never to be acquainted.

'Yes, work,' continued Lexa. 'You could probably earn a little money for yourself.'

Suzanne's mouth twisted. 'What sort of work could I do?'

'I don't know exactly, but in the tourist season, there must be plenty of temporary jobs in hotels, in shops.'

'But here there are no hotels, no shops.'

'Not within a few yards of your house, admitted, but in Sartène there are at least two hotels and a number of shops of one sort and another. Many more in Propriano and——'

Suzanne started laughing. 'Do you think my father would allow me to work in an hotel or a shop in a town?'

'Why not? What's wrong with earning a living? Or at least part of a living?'

Suzanne shook her blonde head. 'You don't understand the Corsicans. A Moriani would never allow his only daughter to mix with all kinds of people to be found in shops.'

Lexa stared at her companion. Several angry phrases jostled in her mind. Finally she said, 'I'm trying very hard

53

not to be rude or offend you, but frankly I think you can't afford such pride nowadays.'

'It is not pride! It is tradition!' Suzanne's voice rose shrilly. 'Do you realise that even now most Corsican girls are careful not to be seen speaking to men who are not their brothers or cousins or some other relative? To go for a walk with such a man means that her honour is lost.'

Lexa smiled. 'Those customs may have been in force a few years ago, but surely not now?'

'My father still lives in the same way as he did when he was young,' declared Suzanne.

'Then how do you manage with Bryden? Have you never walked alone with him?'

Suzanne flushed. 'My father does not always know about our meetings. In any case, I have Philippe to protect me.'

'Well, let's return to the subject of work,' pursued Lexa. 'A little money of your own earned honestly would give you a certain independence.'

'I don't wish to be independent! I want to marry Bryden. Then I shall have my own home and there will be no need for me to work.'

Lexa gave up, but could not resist one final thrust. 'In England, even the daughters of titled fathers, aristocrats, train for some kind of work and make themselves useful.'

'English girls have no shame!' retorted Suzanne. 'They come here for holidays and flaunt themselves in front of men. Even in bikinis, they dance with men, and when they swim, they let men—oh, it is too shocking!' She shuddered in disgust.

Yet it was obvious to Lexa that Suzanne was merely sheltering hypocritically behind old traditions in order to avoid binding herself to a routine of daily work.

'If I'm staying for dinner,' she said, adroitly changing the subject, 'then I ought to telephone Madame Frankland.'

Suzanne smiled blandly. 'No telephone here. Once we had it, but my father forgot to pay the bills and so they took it away.'

'In that case——'

'Don't worry. I'll drive you home safely,' Suzanne reassured her.

Lexa now began to wonder if she had let herself in for a difficult evening. Philippe was almost sure to return for the evening meal, yet she would not ask Suzanne.

As it happened, he did not put in an appearance, so she was relieved, and at the table did her best to enjoy the meal served by the housekeeper, Blanche. The cooking was well below the standard of food served in the Franklands' house under Marguerite's expert French supervision, but although here it was not served attractively, Lexa realised that it was not the typical fare of the mountain peasants. Smoked ham and sausage with raw onions in the local unrefined olive oil, which had a provocative musty flavour; then mutton stew heavily flavoured with garlic accompanied by spiced cabbage and followed by melon and cheese.

The dishes failed to look appetising, but Lexa found them piquant and enjoyable.

'When my mother was here,' Suzanne said towards the end of the meal, 'Blanche was taught to make better meals, in the French style, but now she has gone back to her own kind of cooking.'

'Is it long since you lost your mother?' Lexa asked.

'Five years.' Suzanne shot a wary look at her father across the table and Lexa did not pursue the subject.

After a few moments, Gregorio growled, 'If your mother were here, we'd be eating fancy French food instead of good Corsican stuff.'

His French was heavily accented and difficult for Lexa to follow, but she understood the gist of his remark.

The two girls remained silent until it was time to clear the dishes and plates ready for Blanche to collect. Gregorio retired to a small room next to the kitchen, while Suzanne and Lexa drank their coffee in the sitting-room.

Eventually Lexa rose to go back to Fontenay. 'Do you mind driving at night?' she asked Suzanne.

'Not at all, but it is early yet. You have plenty of time.'

Now the impression struck Lexa with some force that Suzanne was playing for time. Until Philippe returned? That was the obvious explanation, but when another half-hour had elapsed, Lexa became more anxious to go home.

'I really must go now. Madame Frankland will be wondering where on earth I've got to.'

'Or perhaps it is that you are anxious to see Bryden tonight? Otherwise you cannot sleep well?'

Lexa flushed, then was annoyed with herself, for there was simply no reason why any taunt about Bryden should make the slightest impression on her.

'I'm more concerned about the Franklands than about Bryden,' she said testily. 'Please, Suzanne, let's go now.'

The other girl shrugged in her usual French manner. 'Very well. As you wish.'

In the car, Suzanne seemed to have great difficulty in starting. After fidgeting for several minutes, she announced, 'How sorry I am! No good.'

'You mean the car won't go?' queried Lexa, all her anxieties descending on her. 'It was all right when we arrived.'

'But not now.'

'Could your father see to it and put it right?'

'He is not very clever with cars. Better with horses and mules.'

Lexa was coldly angry, convinced now that Suzanne was playing a mean trick on her.

'So what do you suggest? Is it possible for me to walk back to Fontenay?'

Suzanne's derisive laughter rang loudly in the closed atmosphere of the car. 'Walk! That would be madness. The road twists and you would not know the way. You'd be over the mountain edge and never be rescued. That would be a disaster.'

'But I can't sit here all night,' Lexa objected.

'No, but you can stay the night with us. In the morning, Philippe will put right whatever is wrong and he will drive you back.'

Lexa slowly swung herself out of the car. 'I'm more concerned about staying away without letting anyone know.'

'There's no need for worry,' returned Suzanne airily.

'They will guess you are here with us.'

'Or that we might have gone up into the mountains or fallen over a precipice!' Lexa's voice was sharpened with incipient tears. What would the Franklands think of her if she behaved so discourteously at the very beginning of her employment?

'Come, let us go into the house,' invited Suzanne. After some hesitation Lexa followed her, but then she caught the sound of a car and a few moments later the headlights shone into the yard. As the car stopped and a man alighted, Lexa realised that she was in a cleft stick. There was no way of avoiding the prospect that Philippe would drive her home, if not tonight, then tomorrow morning.

Philippe thrust his head through the half-open door of the car, spoke to the driver and then came towards Lexa.

'Lexa! What a pleasant surprise! Have you been here all day?'

'Is it possible for you to take me home tonight?' she asked. She did not relish a tête-à-tête journey with him, but it seemed she had no choice.

'Naturally. It will be my greatest pleasure.'

'Something is wrong with the car,' Suzanne snapped. She was standing in the doorway of the house. 'Lexa can easily stay the night with us. I will prepare a room.'

'Then if the car has broken down,' said Philippe, 'it will be a delight to have you here with us until tomorrow.'

'Philippe,' said Lexa urgently, 'please look at the car. It may be only a trifle, some small gadget gone wrong.'

'But you could stay——'

'Please, Philippe, I insist. It's very important for me to go home tonight and not stay out without the Franklands knowing properly where I am.'

Philippe's arm swung around Lexa's waist. 'Perhaps you're afraid that Bryden will lower his opinion of you if he knows?'

'I'm certain that Mr and Mrs Frankland will not be pleased. See if the car will start. If not, perhaps you could ask——'

The car which had brought Philippe home was already

disappearing out of the courtyard, so there was no solution there.

'It would be quite wrong of us to keep you here against your will, my dear Lexa,' Philippe said softly, his face within inches of her own. 'When you stay with us, I hope it will be because you are eager to be here.'

He walked towards his car and Lexa followed. Five minutes later the engine had started and Lexa wasted no time in seating herself. As he drove towards Fontenay, Philippe said, 'I had no idea that you were spending the day with Suzanne. I would have come home much earlier.'

'It was intended to be only an afternoon,' explained Lexa. 'But Suzanne insisted on my staying to dinner.' There was much more that she wanted to say—that Suzanne had delayed her departure as long as possible so that Philippe would have time to return, and then obviously faked a breakdown in the car, knowing that Lexa was ignorant of motor mechanics.

Philippe's headlights flashed around the curves of the twisting road and Lexa was relieved that she could not see too clearly the hazards of the mountain wall on one side and the sheer drop on the other.

Without exaggerating her attitude, she sat up straight enough to maintain a clear distance between herself and the driver. Philippe needed no encouragement from her to halt suddenly and take her in his arms. Of that she felt sure. The sudden thought occurred to her that if the driver had been Bryden, would her reactions have been the same? In the darkness, her cheeks burned with the knowledge that Bryden's company would have been infinitely more desirable than that of Philippe. She would have relaxed, instead of sitting rigidly, and disregarded how long the journey took or how late the hour.

The lights in the downstairs rooms at Fontenay were still blazing away when Philippe entered the drive and before Lexa had alighted, Edgar and Marguerite were at the front door.

Lexa began her apologies and explanations, but Edgar cut her short with, 'Not to worry. We guessed where you were and that Philippe would eventually bring you home.'

She turned belatedly to thank Philippe, murmured a few words and was then seized in his arms while he kissed her with practised thoroughness.

'It was the utmost pleasure,' he said when he released her. 'One that must be repeated many times.'

She was glad that Edgar and Marguerite had gone indoors and were not witnesses of this midnight scene, but to her dismay she saw that Bryden was standing by the front porch, an interested onlooker. She tried to soothe her own ruffled feelings into a calmer state by bidding Philippe goodnight and waving to him as he drove off in his car.

Almost immediately, she realised that this had been a mistake, for now she had to pass Bryden and was discomfited by the amused expression on his face.

'You seem to have made quite a conquest of Philippe,' he said quietly, knocking the ash off his cigar. 'Or is it that you can both be more open about the affair now that Clifford is no longer on the scene?'

After the protracted struggle to get away from the Moriani house and maintaining a touch-me-not attitude in the car with Philippe, Lexa was emotionally tired, but she could not allow Bryden to mock her. 'There is no "affair", as you call it, between me and Philippe. Surely you understand that he's a volatile Frenchman—or half-Corsican—and he thinks no more of a goodnight kiss and hug than I do.'

'Oh? Does that mean that you dish out goodnight kisses to all and sundry?'

Inward fury shook her so that her lips trembled before she could utter her next words. 'No good ever comes of jumping to conclusions or making snap judgments. Perhaps when I've been here longer and made a few more acquaintanceships—especially with young men,' she added slyly, 'you'll be able to answer that question for yourself. Goodnight!'

She marched past him, head high and hoping he would not notice her flushed cheeks or hear the hammering of her heart. If he had expected to be 'dished out' a goodnight kiss, then she was glad to disappoint him.

Lexa was determined to have as little as possible to do with Bryden. Since he was one of the family, she would have to treat him with conventional courtesy, even though that was difficult enough sometimes, when he showed his particular brand of friendly malice. She told herself that she would be relieved when the daily routine of practice with Gabrielle would start. These odd days intended for pleasure seemed to have an unsettling effect on her.

'One more day of freedom,' announced Edgar next morning to Gabrielle, 'and then you start your daily chores.'

Lexa was standing on the terrace close enough to hear. In that case she would stay at home and attend to her not very extensive stock of dresses. She was halfway up the stairs leading to her room when Gabrielle came running up behind her.

'Do you want to go shopping in Ajaccio?' the girl asked. 'Edgar says we don't have to start work until tomorrow, so it's a good chance.'

Lexa hesitated. 'I could certainly do with one new dress and perhaps a blouse or shirt to wear with trousers, but——'

'All right, that's settled. Will you be ready in ten minutes?'

Gabrielle had already dashed down the stairs and vanished into one of the downstairs rooms before Lexa could reply. As she changed her shoes and picked up a jacket, she wondered who was driving. When she saw Bryden standing by the car and talking to Edgar, she was tempted to make some trivial excuse for not going along with Gabrielle, but at the back of her mind she knew she was being dishonest. She had known the driver would be Bryden and some deep, compulsive urge persuaded her to accept his company when it was offered.

Gabrielle had not yet appeared and now Bryden leaned into the car and sounded his horn. 'I shall go without you, Gaby, if you don't come immediately!' he shouted towards the girl's bedroom window.

Lexa's pulses suddenly leaped at the thought that she

would be alone with Bryden, but she sobered herself, remembering that Marguerite or Edgar might easily be coming, too.

Gabrielle came running out of the house, gave her mother a perfunctory kiss and hurled herself into the back seat of the car.

'That's right,' said Bryden grimly, 'You and Lexa together in the back. I don't want either of you with me in front, and incessantly turning round to chat to each other.'

Gabrielle twisted her face into a monkey grin. 'So polite, my brother!' she said ironically. 'You should learn from Philippe how to be courteous to girls.'

Bryden gave what could only be described as a snort. 'Philippe? Honeyed words and courtly gestures and the tender grace of a goodnight kiss.'

Lexa winced at that unkind cut, but Gabrielle would not understand that he was referring to last night when Philippe had so obviously kissed her before his departure.

When they were nearing Propriano, Gabrielle suggested that Bryden might stop for coffee. 'The Miramar is a good place.'

'I don't want to stop anywhere,' he replied over his shoulder. 'I've business calls to make in Ajaccio and I shall miss the people I want to see. Can't you wait until then?'

'It would only take a couple of minutes!' persisted Gabrielle.

Bryden shouted with derisive laughter. 'A couple of minutes! Half an hour, more like. And then you'd start wandering up the street to peer in some shop we'd passed on the way. You should have asked Sophie for a flask of coffee before we started.'

Gabrielle sighed heavily, then turned towards Lexa. 'Perhaps it is because he is English that he is so disobliging. No! I don't mean that, for you are also English. Maybe it's only the men of your country.'

'Maybe it's because Englishmen aren't always ready to dance attendance on importunate young French girls,' Bryden cut in.

'Importunate?' Gabrielle echoed. 'What does it mean?

What nasty word is he using about me?'

Lexa laughed. 'Not really nasty. Only that you're demanding.'

'Pouf! One might as well demand a favour of the moon as ask for a small mercy from Bryden.'

'You're making heavy weather of it, Gabrielle,' said Bryden. 'What's so special in Propriano?'

By this time he had already driven through most of the town and was on the road heading for Olmeto.

'Too late now, anyway,' grumbled Gabrielle.

'Doesn't matter,' murmured Lexa.

After another mile or so, Bryden said, 'Look, you two. Let me get you into Ajaccio as soon as I can. Then you can do as you like for the rest of the day, have lunch somewhere, spend your time shopping. I'll pick you up at six o'clock, not a minute later, and we can either have dinner in Ajaccio or Propriano or anywhere else you fancy on the way home. Now that's my best offer.'

He spoke to the two girls, Lexa reflected, as though he were a schoolmaster giving two of his pupils a day's outing for a treat.

But Gabrielle clapped her hands together and immediately said, 'Stop at Propriano for dinner. I like it better than Ajaccio.'

He dropped the girls outside a café in one of the main squares of Ajaccio. 'Six o'clock!' he called, as he drove off. 'Not a second later or I'll leave you stranded.'

Gabrielle flung him a contemptuous gesture of dismissal, while Lexa grinned at the disappearing car. 'Now we can have the coffee we're dying for,' Gabrielle suggested.

'Why not lunch now and then we'll be free all the afternoon for the shopping?'

Gabrielle accepted Lexa's suggestion and conducted her companion to a restaurant called La Reine Margot, where they ate a superb lunch beginning with a smooth, rich paté and finishing with a scone-type pancake with lemon served hot on a baked beech leaf.

'Whether I've the energy to traipse around the streets,' complained Lexa, with a laugh, 'I really don't know. You shouldn't have brought me to such a good place.'

'We can be lazy over our coffee for half an hour,' decided Gabrielle. 'Then we'll go.'

Eventually the two girls stirred themselves and Lexa bought a turquoise and white outfit of jacket and trousers with a frilly turquoise nylon blouse. The items were interchangeable with her other clothes and she would have to make them last for a while.

Gabrielle took quite a time to find a long dress for evenings and in the end gave up the search and compromised with a skirt and a white sweater. 'Maman must come with me to find the dress,' she said. 'People in the shops always find something hidden away in the showcases and bring it out for her. Not for me. They think I'm too young!'

Lexa was glad to have an hour or so to spare, for she never tired of the charm of Ajaccio, with its palm-fringed avenues, where statues and monuments everywhere reminded the visitor that here was Napoleon's birthplace. The shopping streets were lively, and attractive squares were often lined with cafés. Best of all, she loved roaming up and down the narrow alleyways of the old fishing town where it seemed that people had time to gossip with each other or chat companionably on the quay, where they mended their nets. Brightly coloured boats, blue, crimson, yellow, bobbed at their moorings and across the sapphire bay the Iles Sanguinaires lay like mauve smudges on the horizon.

But dawdling in the late afternoon sun brought its hazards, for a glance at her watch indicated to Lexa that only five minutes remained before she and Gabrielle ought to be back at the place where Bryden would pick them up.

'It's too warm to hurry!' grumbled Gabrielle as Lexa's longer legs stepped out up the narrow street.

'He threatened to go without us if we weren't punctual.'

'He'll wait.'

Gabrielle's confidence was misplaced, for when the girls arrived, there was no sign of Bryden or his car.

When a quarter of an hour went by, they looked at each other. It was now half-past six, according to the chime of the church clock across the square.

When he drove alongside the pavement, Gabrielle greeted him with a triumphant, 'So *you* were late, not us!'

'You'd better get in quickly before the police nab me. I've had to drive twice round the block. I suppose your watches stopped.'

Gabrielle and Lexa bundled themselves and their parcels into the car without further argument.

'Why couldn't you be punctual?' he demanded as he steered through the rush-hour traffic. 'I sat at that café from ten to six until ten past. I had to drive away then, because I was in a prohibited parking space.'

'Sorry, my dear brother,' replied Gabrielle airily. 'But we're here now and ready for a good dinner at Propriano.'

'I've a good mind to let you whistle for your dinners,' he muttered, 'except that——' he broke off as a motor bike slewed in front of him.

A thought occurred to Lexa. 'Do they know at home that we'll be staying out for dinner?' she asked. 'I wouldn't want to be missing two nights running without anyone knowing.'

'Rest assured that no one will send out a search party for you,' Bryden answered crisply. 'I've already telephoned Sophie.'

Lexa subsided, disheartened by his tone of voice as much as the actual words. Need he go out of his way to trample her down when all she desired was to save other people trouble?

He stopped at a restaurant built on piles over the harbour, but Gabrielle was obviously disappointed. It seemed that she would have preferred one of the other available places.

By the time the meal was finished, the sun had set in a blaze of colour, fiery crimson streaked with yellow and mauve, and the sea held the darkness of twilight.

'You've been remarkably silent during dinner,' remarked Bryden as he stirred his coffee. 'Run out of light conversation?'

'I could probably find enough trivialities to talk about,

but I'd be almost sure to get my head snapped off.' Lexa had not meant to be so blunt in her reply and glanced towards the place where Gabrielle had been sitting, but the girl was not there.

'Then let's try some airy nonsense and see who can win at head-snapping. You're quite competent in that direction yourself, aren't you?'

'I wasn't aware of it. Perhaps only with some people who show me a bad example.'

Bryden laughed. 'If that isn't one of the best slap-downs I've experienced recently!'

'Only because you were eager to wear a cap that fitted,' she retorted.

'Come, let's change to a safer topic. I can see that I shall get the worst of any encounter with you tonight. Tell me, what are your interests besides music?'

Thankfully, she followed his lead to less contentious matters. 'I like reading, of course.'

'What do you read?'

'Oh, all sorts of books. Fiction, travel, biography, plays. I did a season or two with a small amateur drama company in the town where I lived.'

'Ah, so you act. I wonder, then, if it's possible to see your true self.' He was mocking her, but his voice was warmer, without that cold edge of malice.

'All of us act most of the time in our daily lives,' she returned. 'Or so philosophers seem to think.'

'Yes, we wear a mask to hide our true natures, I suppose,' he agreed. 'What kind of parts did you play?'

'Any part that the producer cast me for. We did mostly light comedies, so I was never a tragedy queen. Often, I prompted or stage-managed or made the tea. We all had to make ourselves useful as well as act. The men made the sets or painted scenery. Clifford was in a couple of productions, but he had only limited time.'

'Was he always the hero of the piece?'

'Always!' replied Lexa. 'He'd have been affronted to be given a minor part.'

'You take a realistic view of Clifford?'

'The other things that interest me are travel or nature films on television,' she went on hurriedly, realising her mistake in mentioning Clifford. 'Your father mentioned that he might soon have a commission for the music to a nature film.'

'Yes, he's done several of those.' After a moment Bryden added, 'I think my father will soon cure your liking for that sort of film. By the time you've seen it screened forty or fifty times, you'll be heartily sick of it.'

'Who knows? Now supposing you tell me of your interests apart from property management. What are *your* extra-mural pursuits?'

'Difficult to find much time for any of them.' He sighed with mock gravity. 'My father and I play chess sometimes— when the women of the house will let us have a little peace and quiet. Apart from that, my reading is mostly on architectural subjects. I trained as an architect before I came to live here.'

That was news to Lexa. She imagined he must have had some sort of professional training, but she had not wanted to ask questions about his career.

'But you play tennis and swim,' she remarked. Gabrielle had told her that Bryden was a formidable tennis player and had won a tournament in last year's tennis week in Ajaccio.

'Not much time to practise either.'

'Where's Gabrielle?' she asked. 'She seems to have disappeared.'

'Perhaps she thought it discreet to leave us alone,' he gibed. 'She'd better turn up soon, or I shall go home without her.'

Lexa laughed. 'I don't believe you'd be so callous.'

'Is that a challenge? Careful, or I might ditch you at some future date.'

After a short time, Bryden suggested that they should leave the restaurant. 'Gabrielle is probably not far away.'

By the time he and Lexa had reached the place where he had parked his car, Gabrielle came towards them. She was wearing a pale lemon-coloured dress and Lexa could have sworn that a moment before the French girl had been clasped in a man's arms, the sleeves of his dark jacket folding her closely to him.

'Sit in the front with Bryden,' she said to Lexa. 'I'm dead tired and I might doze.'

Lexa shot a querying glance at Bryden, whose face illumined by the street lights remained completely impassive.

On the last stretch of the homeward journey she concentrated her attention on the seaward view, whenever the coast road afforded glimpses. The lights of Propriano were soon left behind and when the road struck inland towards Sartène, only the craggy walls of rock on both sides were visible in the headlights.

Gabrielle had curled herself up on the back seat and appeared to be fast asleep. In one sense, Lexa would have been gratified to follow Gabrielle's example and at least feign sleep, for she would have been separated from Bryden. Now his nearness had its most disquieting effect on her. She was too aware of his masculine magnetism for her own comfort. Perversely, she longed for the journey to continue for ever and at the same time would be glad when it was over. She stared ahead, scolding herself for her weakness in allowing such foolish emotions to master her. Surely she should be able to exercise more control over the wild fancies that floated through her mind. She refused to allow herself to examine those wild fancies, for apparently she was no wiser than Suzanne, who was at least some three years younger.

Bryden had driven through the town of Sartène and was along the narrow road that led towards Tizzano and the coast before Lexa was aware of the fact. Ten minutes later he was turning through the gates of Fontenay and brought the car to a stop, not outside the front door, but nearer to the garages.

Gabrielle, who was wide awake now, clambered out, taking some of her parcels with her, and Lexa opened the door her side, prepared to follow suit. Bryden laid his hand on her wrist and his touch sent fire into her veins.

'In a hurry?' he queried. 'Surely I'm entitled to one of

your brand of goodnight kisses?'

'No, Bryden, I don't——'

But his arms were around her, he drew her close to him and kissed her with an intensity that at first surprised her, then caused her to reciprocate with passionate fervour. In the bliss of the moment all thought was suspended. It was only when he released her that she was shocked into the realisation that she had given herself away so completely that nothing would ever be the same again between her and Bryden.

'Glad I'm admitted into the charmed circle,' he was saying coolly. 'I don't take kindly to other men enjoying favours denied to me.'

She scrambled out of the car, ashamed, humiliated, reached into the back for her shopping packages and ran without another word towards the front door.

She raced up the stairs without stopping and was thankful that no one else was about or could waylay her before she reached the refuge of her room. There, she flung herself down on the bed, clenched her fists with rage and wished that she could cry. No tears would ever heal the wounding hurt that Bryden had dealt her tonight. No other man had ever treated her in this cynical fashion, encouraging her to a display of feeling merely to provide himself with amusement. She determined fiercely that no man, least of all Bryden, would ever have the chance again.

CHAPTER FOUR

GABRIELLE and Lexa settled into the practice routine that Edgar had planned—a session of three hours in the morning, with a break in the middle for coffee; time for a siesta after lunch, then a further two hours. After five o'clock or so, Lexa was free until after dinner when she might be required to accompany either Gabrielle or Marguerite, sometimes both, in the drawing-room, but that was not so much hard practice as relaxation in a musical manner.

Three days had gone by since Lexa's trip to Ajaccio and the incident in the car with Bryden, a happening she would prefer to forget. Bryden had gone to the north of the island and was to be away several days, so that his absence helped.

Gabrielle was turning over the pages of a volume of violin and piano sonatas, when she glanced up suddenly at Lexa. 'You can keep secrets?' she queried.

'Usually. Why?'

'I might need you to help me.' Gabrielle had lowered her voice almost to a whisper, although there was little likelihood of conversation being overheard in this practice studio at the end of the modern wing of the house.

Lexa waited, slightly uncomfortable, for she wondered what sort of confidence Gabrielle was about to disclose.

'I have a friend in Propriano,' began Gabrielle.

'A boy-friend?' queried Lexa, although she already guessed the gender.

'Naturally. He works in a hotel, so it's not easy for me to see him often.'

'Is he Corsican or French?'

'No, Italian. From Naples. His name is Stefano and he is very handsome.'

'And he's the man you went to see the other night when we were having dinner in Propriano?'

Gabrielle nodded. 'I had to slip away for a few minutes.'

'Do your parents know about this—friendship?'

'Oh, no! Edgar has given me strict orders that I must not think about men or love or even flirtations for two years. Two years! It is like a prison sentence.'

'But Edgar—and your mother—have your happiness in mind. You do want a professional career in music, don't you?'

'Yes, of course, but it would be nicer to have a little gaiety sometimes.'

Lexa sighed. 'You want your cake and eat it, too. Well, what am I supposed to do?'

Gabrielle moved closer. 'You can help me to see Stefano

69

more often. Oh, it is quite harmless, I assure you.'

'That night—when we arrived at the car—you were in his arms. You're sure it's all harmless?'

'Indeed, yes. Now you know that on Fridays I go to my professor in Sartène. He lives in Ajaccio, but he comes once a week to the music studio in Sartène. Other days he goes to different towns, of course. Stefano tries to take his day off also on Fridays, and he comes from Propriano to meet me. If you also came to Sartène with me every week, you could be my chaperone, and then Stefano and I could slip away somewhere quiet.'

Lexa almost laughed at this naïve absurdity, but she was not anxious to hurt the other girl's young and tender feelings.

'But who drives you into Sartène every week?'

'Oh, sometimes Edgar or my mother. Bryden if he is handy. Or Robert.'

Robert was the husband of Sophie, the housekeeper, and looked after the gardens and all the outside work of the house.

'But whoever drives—do they wait for your lesson to finish?' asked Lexa.

'Oh, no, that's not the case. It is a long class—we don't play for only half an hour—but sit there to listen to other students.'

'I see. A master class.'

'Yes. But it happens that sometimes when we have played our particular pieces, we may go away for a while. That is when I meet Stefano, if I can.'

'But, Gabrielle, this is cheating. Your mother and your stepfather are paying for your lessons from this professor and expect you to profit by them—not go wandering off with the first handsome Italian you meet.'

'When you meet Stefano, you will change your ideas,' said Gabrielle grimly. 'In fact you will probably fall in love with him yourself and I shall lose him.'

'I'll promise not to do that.' An easy promise, thought Lexa, for her heart was so full of Bryden that there was no space left for any other man, however handsome or vivacious. 'Now, you want me to cover up for you while you slide out of part of your lesson. I can't do it, Gabrielle. I'd be cheating, too.'

A slow tear fell down Gabrielle's cheek. 'It is only for the summer,' she pleaded. 'Stefano works in the hotel only while the tourists are here.'

'And then he goes back to Naples—and forgets all about you.'

'He would never forget me,' protested Gabrielle.

'But there's no question of your marrying him. You're too young, anyway, you've your career—and probably he isn't the right man for you.'

'Oh, it isn't marriage! Stefano has no money except what he earns——'

'Then why are you wasting your time?' Lexa was filled with a creeping dread of the future for this lovely girl still only on the threshold of womanhood, yet ready to jeopardise her career, perhaps her whole life, for a summer flirtation.

Gabrielle smiled and blinked away her tears. 'Because it is so delightful to be loved.'

Lexa experienced a catch in the throat when she heard Gabrielle's softly spoken words. Here was the ring of truth from a young, inexperienced girl, and who could deny such a universal principle?

'Look, Gabrielle, I'll try to help you in any way I can, but not anything underhand. I could be your chaperone, but in that case, you'd have to explain to your mother why you need one. Couldn't you invite Stefano to the house on some occasion? Then there would be no need for such secrecy when you meet him at other times.'

Gabrielle shook her head. 'Maman would not approve of him and Edgar would say he is a distraction for me, upsetting to my music.'

Lexa sighed. 'Well, we'll think about it and see what can be arranged.'

The two girls started practice again and Lexa's accurate ear for pitch detected numerous mistakes in Gabrielle's playing. 'C sharp,' she said, pointing to the score, 'and in that passage, you don't get the time quite right. It goes like this'—she played the piano accompaniment then the violin melody.

'Sorry,' murmured Gabrielle, and tucked her violin under her chin and picked up her bow.

But it was evident that the girl's mind was not on the job in hand. Lexa said smoothly, 'Shall we try something else today? You're not quite here.'

'No,' admitted Gabrielle candidly. 'I'm with Stefano and at this moment my music is not so important to me.'

'Then if we skip the rest of today's routine, will you put in extra time tomorrow?'

Gabrielle agreed perfunctorily, but Lexa was determined to see that her companion did not slack next day.

'Today you can dream of Stefano,' she said now briskly, 'but tomorrow we will both work together and think of nothing but strict tempo, the right notes and try to express what the composer had in mind.'

When Gabrielle had gone from the practice studio, Lexa leafed through a pile of piano music, found quantities of works by Grieg, Schubert, Delius and the Spanish composers, Albeniz and Granados. She spent the next hour or more in concentrated practice. She considered that her piano-playing skill had deteriorated considerably in the last few months, with fewer opportunities, so now was her chance to improve. When she returned to England, she ought to be much more accomplished than when she had first come to Corsica.

Her fingers idled on the piano keys. When I go back? The idea was like a knell. Return to England meant that she would probably never see Bryden again and she would have to take up the threads of her life without him.

She plunged into Grieg's 'Papillon', striking wrong notes, aware of the discord that was now her everyday companion.

About a week later, Edgar said at lunch, 'Tomorrow after dinner we'll have a small recital, Gabrielle, and see how you've worked. You can make up your own programme, if that's agreeable to Lexa.'

Consternation flitted across Gabrielle's face. 'But it's

Friday and I go to Sartène for my lesson,' she objected.

'Well, you don't stay to have your dinner in the studio there. You'll be home here in time, no doubt.'

Gabrielle gave Lexa a wary glance, and Lexa guessed that Gabrielle had made a rendezvous with the handsome Stefano.

'I'll send Robert to bring you home a little earlier if you can get your release from the class,' promised Edgar.

Gabrielle bowed her head and studied her plate, defeated and too young to think of some quick way to solve the situation. After the meal was over, she called Lexa and suggested they should walk on the far side of the garden.

'What shall I do, Lexa?' she entreated. 'I promised to meet Stefano at the café where we always go.'

'At what time?'

'Four o'clock. Usually, I can't leave the studio until half-past three, although we are all supposed to stay until half-past four.'

Lexa was silent for a few moments. 'What time does Robert, or whoever is the driver, come to fetch you?'

'Half-past five. Edgar said he'll send Robert there at four o'clock.'

'Well, Stefano will have to miss you for once.'

'But, Lexa, he comes from Propriano. It is his only free time on Fridays.'

'Then the only thing to do is to prevent him wasting his time tomorrow,' said Lexa emphatically. 'You could either telephone him and explain or——'

'I am desolated not to see him,' lamented Gabrielle.

'Just for once, he can do without you—so you can learn to do without him. It isn't the end of the world.'

'It's catastrophe. Once I have let him down, he'll not have faith in me.'

After a long argument, Gabrielle agreed that she would telephone Stefano at the hotel where he worked. 'But one day you must come to Sartène with me and meet him, Lexa. Then you'll understand how much I adore him.'

'When will you 'phone him?' asked Lexa.

'Tomorrow in Sartène. Usually I go out to lunch with

several of the other students. We have only from twelve until one o'clock, so we have to go to a quick snack bar. I can telephone then.'

'Not from here, I suppose, in case someone overheard you?'

'The acoustics of our hall where the telephone is placed are so good that you can hear every word in the kitchen, up the stairs and along the landings. Edgar has an extension in his own studio, but I daren't use that.'

Since Gabrielle was in Sartène most of Fridays, Lexa had a free day.

'Would you be too busy, Lexa, to spend an hour or two in my studio this afternoon?' Edgar asked her during the morning next day. 'I've corrected some pages of the score of a trio I've been working on. If you could manage to make a fair copy, I'd be obliged. But don't work on it longer than you want to.'

Lexa was eager to concentrate on work that would divert her from thinking too much of Gabrielle's difficulties today. 'I could put in an hour or two this morning as well, if you like,' she offered.

'Thanks very much.'

Lexa studied the pages and soon realised that it would be no easy task to decipher Edgar's original notes, his innumerable corrections, or whether the small smudgy marks were intended as notes or were chance blots.

She worked diligently until lunch, sometimes trying out bars on the piano to test if she had interpreted what she thought was correct. But the work was intensely interesting and she applied herself again in the afternoon. She was so absorbed in the intricacies of the work that she did not hear someone enter the studio.

'Trying your hand at composition?' Bryden's voice startled her and she swung round from the piano.

'I don't aspire that high,' she said. 'This is your father's work.'

He came and stood close to her, peering at the sheet of music score in her hand, and she willed herself to remain calm in spite of her racing pulses. As she sat, her head was only a hair's breadth from his chest; one swift turn on her part would bring her against his heart.

'And you really understand all those pothooks? What does that curving line there mean?'

'That you play the notes as a phrase, without breaks between.'

As he pointed to the score, his left hand rested on her shoulder and his touch caused in her the wildest longings so that she had to hold herself rigidly to prevent herself from twisting to throw herself into his arms.

He straightened up and moved away and she was thankful. 'I came to look for my father. I thought he was here. Otherwise I wouldn't have disturbed you.'

Disturbed her! He must never know how much even his presence in the room disturbed her.

'You'll probably find him in the garden.' With a great effort she controlled her voice, although in her own ears it sounded jerky and forced.

'Right. I'll leave you to your blobs and blotches.' As he went out and shut the door, Lexa breathed a sigh of relief. She really must train herself not to fall into a schoolgirl fluster every time Bryden came near her.

She settled again at the table and continued with the fair copy of the score. After more than an hour when she began checking her copy with the original, she found that she had omitted one whole stave, the cello part. Since it involved copying the whole page again, she was furious with herself, for the omission had occurred just at the point where Bryden had interrupted her.

There was nothing for it but to start that page again, and she was still working when Edgar came up to see how she had progressed.

'I'm afraid I've been rather slow,' she apologised, unwilling to disclose her omission.

'Oh, no! You've done very well, considering my awful musical scrawl. Leave it for now and you can do some more in your spare time. No hurry.'

He put down the score sheets on the table and sat in an armchair by the window. Lexa glanced across at him, trying to judge how much Bryden resembled his father. Edgar was not so tall as his son and his build was slighter. The features were similar, allowing for difference in age, but Lexa wondered if Bryden would ever acquire the kindly look that always rested in Edgar's eyes and around his humorous mouth. Not even when Bryden's hair had silvered at the temples as his father's now could Lexa visualise him following Edgar's tolerant, genial mould.

'Bryden tells me, Lexa, that you're interested in nature films. Short ones for television and so on. Is that right?'

'Yes. I am.'

He turned towards her. 'I shall shortly have a commission to do the music for a couple of wild life films. I did several two or three years ago. I thought you might be able to help me.'

'Of course, but in what way?'

Edgar laughed. 'It may become rather boring for you. We fix up a projector and a screen in my study, but the repetition becomes very tedious. By the time the music is finished, I feel I've seen only one film in my whole life and I dream of dancing ducks or flying foxes.'

'I think I could put up with it,' she said with a smile. 'I've often admired the way the music matches the antics of the animals or birds.'

'You should be a good critic then of my efforts.' He gave her an encouraging smile. 'Put away all the work now. You need to relax if you and Gabrielle are entertaining us tonight.'

At dinner Gabrielle appeared composed, so Lexa imagined that the girl had successfully stalled off her admirer, but when the music was being arranged and Lexa queried quietly, 'Did you arrange it?' Gabrielle shook her head.

'I couldn't get in touch by telephone, so I had to leave a message at the café. But his journey will be wasted.'

'That might not do him much harm,' was Lexa's reply.

Edgar had previously explained to Lexa that Gabrielle was required to perform minor recitals, with himself and her mother as audience, plus anyone else who happened to be in the house.

'We don't have them at any fixed period, but usually somewhere between ten days and a fortnight, and I give her very little notice. She must become accustomed to playing at concerts at short notice and also to the formal atmosphere when she plays to a large audience.'

It seemed an excellent idea, thought Lexa at the time, but tonight she would have preferred Bryden to be absent. Confusion might make her play badly and an indifferent accompanist is of no help to a soloist.

Gabrielle had written out her chosen programme and handed it to Edgar first, then to her mother.

'I thought you might play something, Maman. "The Swan", perhaps?'

'Certainly,' agreed Marguerite. 'I'm sure Lexa would know that accompaniment.'

Gabrielle and Lexa began with a Brahms sonata, followed by Beethoven's 'Spring' Sonata No. 5. Marguerite played the beautiful cello piece from Saint-Saens' *Carnival of the Animals*. Then there was an interval.

To Lexa's surprise and, perhaps, resentment, Bryden did not stay after dinner to listen to the music. No doubt the classics were above his head. In one way she was glad that his presence did not have the usual unsettling effect on her, thus spoiling her concentration. Yet she was aware that without him, there was a flatness in the atmosphere.

When they resumed their places, Lexa and Gabrielle played another sonata, this by Grieg, followed by a Gypsy andante from Dohnanyi.

Edgar and Marguerite applauded and smiled at the girls. 'But, Lexa, you must also play us a solo,' suggested Marguerite.

Lexa hardly knew why she chose Grieg's 'Papillon', except that she had recently been practising it, but while her fingers coped with the trills and chords, part of her mind was occupied with images of Bryden. Did he regard all girls as butterflies? Creatures to be admired, chased, caught and freed? Or did he like to add them to his collection? She realised how little she knew of this enigmatic young man who kept her at arm's length when it suited him or gave her a meaningless kiss at the end of an evening. That kiss may have meant nothing to him, in fact she was sure about that, but he had wrecked her world in those few swift moments, for he had incited her to reveal the strength of her own affection for him.

She finished the piece and Edgar rose to clasp her shoulder in a friendly gesture. 'That was well played,' he complimented her.

Gabrielle laughed. 'He hasn't given *me* any praise yet,' she complained.

'Now you shall have my comments.' He seated himself beside his stepdaughter, tucked her violin under his chin and picked up the bow. He selected passages where he thought she could improve her fingering or bowing technique and the girl gave him her whole attention. Lexa reflected on how lucky Gabrielle was to have such an accomplished musician available in her own home.

But then that was part of the outcome of Marguerite's marriage to Edgar. Lexa had learned by now that Marguerite had been widowed for more than ten years and love of music had drawn her and Edgar together. Bryden's mother had died nine years ago, when he was twenty.

'It was a godsend that my father had his musical life to sustain him,' Bryden had said. 'Otherwise, I think he would have gone mad with grief.'

'She was musical, too?' Lexa had asked.

'Not professionally, not like Marguerite. She could strum on the piano, sing a little in a sweet and charming voice, but she was the centre of his life, the reason why he wanted to succeed. Call it inspiration, if you like.' Then he had muttered under his breath and Lexa had only faintly caught the words '... inspiration ... a great thing in a man's life.'

When Lexa was in bed that night, Gabrielle knocked and entered the room.

'I tried so many times to phone Stefano,' she began, 'but he wasn't there. I thought perhaps he had already come early to Sartène.'

'Perhaps he was unable to come at all today.'

'Then he won't get my message at the café.' Gabrielle paced about the room, then sat on the foot of Lexa's bed. 'I was so unhappy. I didn't think I could bear to play. In fact I nearly told Edgar that I didn't feel well.'

'His answer would have been that unless you were ill in bed, you would have to fulfil your engagement, just as in the professional world.'

'I know. Edgar is hard on me.'

'Actually, you played much better tonight than I've ever heard you in rehearsal.' Lexa smiled sympathetically at the younger girl. 'Perhaps a little sorrow is good for one's art?'

Gabrielle laughed. 'Lexa, you are everybody's comforter. Perhaps you should do something to cheer Bryden up.'

'Bryden? Why does he want cheering up?'

Gabrielle gave her very French shrug of the shoulders. 'I think he is unhappy—maybe over a girl.'

Lexa's heart sank like a stone. 'A girl?' she echoed.

'Maybe Suzanne. She adores him, as you can see. In fact she tells everyone. Bryden is fond of her, I know, but I can't be sure if he wants to marry her.'

'What would be the obstacle?' asked Lexa in a dry voice.

Gabrielle sighed. 'Bryden does not seem lucky with girls. When he finds one he wants to marry, something happens to them.'

'What sort of things?'

'Terrible things. Two years ago, soon after Maman married Edgar, Bryden was engaged. One night he and his fiancée were in a party and all went swimming in a pool. The girl was drowned.'

'Oh!' Lexa's face creased with sympathy. 'What a tragic thing to happen!'

'Before then,' went on Gabrielle, 'there was another girl —although I've only been told about this, I didn't know her. She was killed in an air crash. It was a small private plane, only three people in it.'

'Poor Bryden!' murmured Lexa.

'So perhaps now he's not too eager to propose marriage in case——'

'I doubt whether Suzanne would have any fears. If she

knew of these former accidents, I daresay she'd risk her future.' *As I would risk mine!* The thought darted into Lexa's mind with fiery intensity.

When Gabrielle had returned to her own room, Lexa was left sleepless, a tangle of ideas mixed up in her consciousness. Was that why Bryden adopted his air of careless indifference to girls, to love, yet snatched a momentary caress to satisfy his masculine desires?

Early next morning Gabrielle came rushing into Lexa's room. 'Edgar says he's planning a trip to the mountains. We can be away for three or four days. He'll take us both, he says.'

Lexa set aside her breakfast tray with the coffee and rolls. 'Three or four days? What about your practice?'

Gabrielle grinned. 'It's a reward for being a good girl last night and playing not too badly. Shall I tell him you'll go?'

'Of course. How can I bear to practise accompaniments without my lovely solo violinist?'

Gabrielle bent down to give Lexa an affectionate hug. At the door she turned to say, 'Pack a small case and a warm sweater or jacket. It can be cold up there.'

Lexa had already sampled one or two mountain trips when Clifford had been here, but they had not ventured far into the peaks.

Half an hour later, Lexa was downstairs. Evidently Marguerite was not accompanying the party. Then Lexa realised that Bryden was to be driver. Good news? Bad news? Perhaps both.

'It's really a business trip,' Bryden explained, 'and I'm taking Father and you two girls as ballast, so I have to try to keep to an itinerary, or we shall be camping out for about six weeks if I get sidetracked.'

'I'll do my best not to deviate,' Lexa told him coolly.

His eyes flashed a look of amusement, but she turned away quickly.

'How far are we going?' asked Gabrielle.

'As far as Corte, I hope, although not in one day, as I have calls to make and they can be quite lengthy.'

'We might go across to the west of the island and come home by Porto,' suggested Edgar.

'Yes, we could do that,' agreed Bryden.

The car was filled with luggage and stout shoes, a sweater belonging to Bryden stuffed in one corner of the back seat. On the roof were two fishing rods. Did Bryden fish? Lexa wondered. Or was it only Edgar who indulged in such a slow, patient pastime?

The party set out with many injunctions from Marguerite and inquiries as to essential articles.

After Sartène, Bryden took the road that led inland and soon the mountain peaks came into view, rising tier above tier like pinnacles of pale grey granite. After some miles, Bryden took a narrow, twisting track until a small village appeared.

'My first business call,' he announced. 'Would you like to come in with us, Lexa? Gabrielle can wait in the car.'

'There are some island customs which you might like to see,' Edgar added to Lexa.

She accompanied the two men to a small stone building which appeared to be the village inn. A middle-aged man came out to greet Edgar and Bryden and Lexa was introduced as 'our English friend'.

The interior of the inn was dark but comfortably furnished and Lexa was handed a glass of white wine with a delicate flavour. Bryden, Edgar and the innkeeper sat at a large wooden table, where they were joined in a few minutes by two other men. At first, she was slightly embarrassed by the idea of being an eavesdropper, but as the conversation proceeded, she realised that although Bryden and Edgar both spoke mostly in French, the others used what she knew now to be the Corsican dialect, of which she could not understand a word.

Presently the innkeeper's wife came to sit with Lexa, proffering a small, sweet cake on a handsome plate painted with an elaborate design of fruit and flowers.

Lexa spoke in French which the woman undoubtedly understood, but made her replies in the dialect, which left the girl at a complete loss. So the conversation became jerky, then flagged altogether.

The business between the Franklands and the other three men seemed to take a long time with much argument, and at one point apparently reached deadlock. Bryden rose, walked towards the window, then turned to the other men, who all began talking at once, then finally shrugged their shoulders. Whether that signified acceptance or refusal of whatever terms were offered, Lexa had no idea.

Bryden sat down and scrawled figures on several sheets of paper, which the men passed round from hand to hand and studied intently. Finally, there was evidently agreement, nodding heads and clasped hands to seal the bargain.

Bryden came across to Lexa. 'I'm sorry you've had to wait so long. In these parts, business talks can't be hurried.'

'Oh, I was fascinated by the discussions going on, especially as I couldn't understand a word of it. Were you buying or selling?'

He laughed. 'Not exactly either, but both. We'll tell you more about it later in the day.'

Outside, Gabrielle was sitting at a table under a couple of trees. She had been served with a glass of wine and now the innkeeper's wife hurried out with glasses and a large flask of red wine to serve the men.

'What about you, Lexa?' Edgar asked, the flask poised over an empty glass in front of her.

'I've already had one glass of white wine.'

'Then try this very good red,' he invited, and poured her a generous measure. 'It's *our* wine, so you need not stint yourself.'

'*Your* wine?'

'It's our inn,' Edgar explained. 'Bryden bought it last year, but we haven't altered the way it's run.'

'Except to make it slightly profitable!' put in Bryden.

'Yes, of course. Left to me, I'd lose money every year.'

'You'd be robbed every year,' added his son drily.

The innkeeper's wife came out carrying a parcel wrapped in paper and tied with red string. Bryden accepted the package with smiles, but without surprise.

When they had driven away from the inn, Edgar explained

to Lexa, 'It's a cheese. When discussions take place and the deal or the arrangement is concluded, a gift is always added to whatever is bought or sold. In season, it might be a melon or a dozen freshly picked oranges.'

'What an interesting custom!' Lexa commented. 'But what did you buy or sell?'

Bryden laughed. 'Nothing, actually. All we have to do is arrange for one man to supply olive oil to that inn, for another to provide it with sausages and so on. In return, the innkeeper will supply others with wine or oranges. He has the vineyards and orange groves, others keep the sheep or goats. It's almost a form of barter still practised.'

'But surely some money must change hands?'

'Oh, yes, but only for the particular produce that is needed.'

'It sounds as though it would become a complicated muddle.'

Bryden shook his head. 'On the contrary, it's very simple and straightforward because everyone understands the system.'

'And no one cheats—or gets cheated?' Lexa queried with a smile.

The two men laughed. 'When Corsicans try cheating each other,' Edgar pointed out, 'the fur and feathers fly. Vendettas have started from trivial swindles. But of course, it's legitimate to cheat us and other nationalities if the chance arises. On the whole, we find them no worse than anyone else.'

At the next village the party stopped for lunch. Here, in addition to the inn, there was a cluster of small villas or chalets built for holiday tourists who wanted to be in the heart of the mountains and near the river for fishing. They had only recently been completed and some were already occupied, but Bryden chose one that was still empty and suggested that Lexa might like to glance over the interior.

'These chalets are one of your pet schemes, I understand,' she said as he showed her the accommodation, one bedroom, a small living-room with a balcony, and a well-equipped kitchen and bathroom.

'These places are fairly small,' he remarked, 'but the kind of people who come here for climbing and fishing don't need palatial apartments. Otherwise, they'd stay down in the coastal resorts. Also, to build large structures would be quite out of keeping with the surroundings.'

Lexa remembered Suzanne's complaint that Bryden opened shops in competition with her father in the same villages and now she gazed around when she stepped outside the villa. In one corner was a small shop and Bryden began walking towards it. 'And this is one of the shops which you run in opposition to Suzanne's father?' Lexa asked.

'Who told you that? Philippe?' he demanded brusquely.

'No. Suzanne. She said that you take away her father's trade.'

Bryden laughed. 'Trade? What trade did he ever have? Poor little shacks selling stale provisions or the dregs of the wine vats and charging high prices. All his life he's had the chance to make them successful, but usually all he's wanted to do is leave matters in the hands of a local man and then collect what profit he could, without bothering to find out what people really wanted to buy. As soon as someone else comes along, he laments that he's pushed out of business.'

Lexa could see that Bryden's reasoning was probably justified, but she felt obliged to put in a word for the Moriani family. 'But when someone has been established for a long time, it's always sad to be ousted by a newcomer.'

Bryden glanced at her and she was aware of a sharp leaping of her senses, which she tried her best to flatten.

'So those two have convinced you that I'm the bold tycoon out to ruin them. If Philippe had ever had any energy, he could have helped his father a good deal and done exactly what my father and I have done in the past couple of years. But he's incurably lazy—except when it comes to chasing the girl of the moment.'

Lexa flushed. That was a dig at her, of course, but she would not give Bryden the satisfaction of knowing that his jibe had gone home.

After lunch when the business transactions with the inn

had taken place, Bryden drove still farther northward where the high maquis was sometimes interrupted by grassy parklands and clumps of holm oak. Chestnut trees grew out of the bracken and now the leaves were bright green.

'In the autumn,' remarked Gabrielle, 'the chestnuts look gorgeous, all gold and copper colours. You must stay until the autumn, Lexa, if only to see the chestnuts.'

Lexa smiled, but made no reply. She knew, now, that if she saw chestnuts in their autumn glory anywhere else, she would immediately remember Bryden and long for his presence.

At Ghisoni, Bryden stopped to discuss the next part of the route with his father. 'I don't know whether to turn off here and go along the river valley, then turn left up to Vezzani, or keep straight on the main road and then turn off.'

'The main road would be shorter,' replied Edgar, studying the map, 'but probably the road to Vezzani is not so good.'

'I'll try it,' decided Bryden. 'I want enough time to call at our place there, and then be able to catch our suppers.'

'To catch our suppers?' echoed Lexa, turning to Gabrielle, who grinned, then explained, 'Edgar and Bryden always believe that the trout are just waiting for them to come along and hook them. What shall we do if you don't catch enough fish?' The question was directed towards the two men.

Edgar turned round towards the girls. 'Starve. Good for the figure to miss a meal sometimes.'

Lexa had realised that at some point in the journey the men would use the angling tackle they had brought, but she had not imagined that their direct purpose would be to provide a meal.

The call at the inn at Vezzani took longer than Bryden had intended, apparently, and while the two men were occupied Lexa roamed about the main street with its tall stone houses, red-tiled roofs glowing in the sun.

She returned to the car just as Bryden emerged from the inn. 'There's time to watch the sunset,' he told her. 'But not here. A little way outside the village.'

She had watched several colourful sunsets from various parts of the coast, but at the point where Bryden stopped the sight was one to remember. Jagged spikes of granite were flooded with rose and orange between chasms of violet. The valley, thickly forested, was bathed in golden light while the shadowed side appeared deep sea blue.

The colours on the mountains changed from minute to minute, ranging from amber to crimson, then to purple, until the lower slopes were blurred and fading, but the topmost peaks still glowed with fire, spearing up into the sky like icebergs.

Lexa remained standing outside the car, unwilling to shatter the silence with even a murmur of appreciation. The valley became grey-green and sombre, the road ahead was blue-shadowed and the fire on the peaks diminished to crimson tips.

'Ready to go, Lexa?' Bryden's quiet voice roused her from what was almost a trance and as she turned, his arm rested for an instant on her shoulder. The fire in her blood was equivalent to the fire that had glowed on the mountains and as she closed her eyes for a moment, she realised that she must school her turbulence to be as transient as the flush on the peaks.

The inn where the four would stay the night was small, stone-built and overlooked the river and as soon as Bryden drove up to the entrance he was unloading his fishing tackle, while Edgar conducted the two girls into the inn and eventually to their rooms.

'No luxuries here,' commented Gabrielle, 'but up here in the mountains, everything is very clean.'

'You've stayed here before?' queried Lexa, punching the bed to feel its springiness.

'Not this particular inn, but others. Always the best food is in these villages, really Corsican food.'

But Lexa was not to sample the good Corsican food tonight, for she and Gabrielle were commanded to go down to the river bank where Bryden was already casting his line.

'Make yourselves useful, you two,' he ordered. 'Get the

fire going.'

Edgar came along with an armful of brushwood which he proceeded to place in a criss-cross pattern, then set a match to the pile.

There was a shout from Bryden as he landed the first trout. Edgar took the leaping, struggling fish from the net while Bryden was attending to baiting his hook.

'Here, Lexa.' Edgar handed her a couple of pointed sticks as he placed the fish on top of the wood fire. 'When it's done one side, turn it over with these sticks.'

She had never before taken part in a fish picnic and was delighted with this new experience. In the space of another ten minutes Bryden had landed half a dozen trout. Edgar dealt with the cleaning while Gabrielle and Lexa turned the fish.

'I think we have enough!' Edgar called to his son. 'Leave some fish in the river for someone else.'

Lexa had been amazed at the rate of Bryden's catch.

'Have you some special magic that fish come to your bait when you whistle?' she asked.

He was squatting on his haunches, uncorking a large bottle of wine and he gave her an oblique, teasing glance. 'I'm irresistible—as a fisherman, of course. Trout come rushing up as soon as my line touches the water, they push each other out of the way for the pleasure of being caught.'

Edgar was shaking out a white cloth to lay on the grassy bank. 'Don't listen to him, Lexa. There are so many trout and other fish in these mountain rivers that you could easily scoop them up with your hands as they go by. They don't need an angler.'

Bryden made a grimace at his father. 'Thank you, Father,' he mocked. 'Lexa can cut me down to size quite effectively without you aiding and abetting her.'

Lexa opened her mouth to protest that she had not intended to disparage Bryden's efforts to provide them with supper, but Edgar was already dishing out the baked trout on paper plates, while Gabrielle was handing small bread rolls.

'Eat while the fish is hot,' advised Edgar, as he cut

chunks of his own portion with a knife and used his fingers as a fork.

Lexa followed the example of the others, although Bryden used no knife, but picked up his fish and gnawed lumps from the bones. 'The only way to eat freshly-cooked trout,' he said. 'Natural and uncivilised.'

Edgar poured the wine into stone mugs and it tasted deliciously cool.

By the time the meal was finished and the debris disposed of, darkness had filled the valley and only a gleam of light remained in the west above the mountains. Lexa lay full length on the river bank, listening to the sound of the torrent as it gushed and murmured over the rocks below.

Her mind was not so relaxed as her body, for turbulent chaotic thoughts roamed about inside her head. She was so determined not to succumb to Bryden's magnetism and yet his very nearness almost overcame her rigid endeavours. She was now comforted by the fact that in the presence of Edgar and Gabrielle she was forced to behave as though Bryden meant no more to her than if he had been a beloved brother.

'Have you heard from Clifford lately?' Bryden's quiet voice startled her and as she turned to face the spot where she supposed him to be, she realised that Edgar and Gabrielle were no longer close by.

'We agreed not to write to each other,' she answered after a lengthy pause. She had to adjust herself to a circumstance that included Clifford, a far-away subject now.

'Self-denying—on both sides,' he murmured. 'Your suggestion or his?'

'Both,' she said tersely.

In the darkness she could hear him laugh softly. 'I'm sorry if the mere mention of him upsets you.'

'It doesn't,' she retorted.

'Oh, come, Lexa, you can't be as hard as that, surely?' In the dimness she could just discern his face, his shoulders as he lay on his back. 'I think it was a very good scheme of yours.'

'Scheme? What do you mean?'

'You know perfectly well. You send Clifford home, you tell him not to write, you deprive him of your own letters, knowing that a short separation is going to make him more keen than ever.'

'More keen for what?'

'To marry you, of course.'

She sat up straight, her body tense. 'He might be just as keen to forget me altogether. Out of sight, out of mind is just as valid as the one about absence making the heart grow fonder.'

'All the same, deep down, you know that eventually you'll return to England and take up where you left off.'

'You're quite wrong,' she said warmly. 'Clifford is free of me and he has the right to please himself.'

'And you, Lexa?'

'Why do you keep probing? I don't ask inquisitive questions about your love life or ferret about to find out which girl you might want to marry—if indeed marriage happens to come within your sphere.'

She immediately regretted that last impulsive phrase, remembering what Gabrielle had told her about Bryden's misfortunes with his girl-friends.

'It could be that, as you say, marriage doesn't come within my sphere. Perhaps I'm not cut out for it.' His tone had become sombre, as though his thoughts were filled with lost dreams.

Lexa remained silent, aware of the unceasing longing that occupied her and would not be assuaged except by Bryden's love. Here in this spot, high in the mountains and under a starlit sky, with this man at her side, within reach if she stretched out her hand only a few inches, the night should have been romantic. But he had erected a formidable barrier between himself and her, deliberately reminding her of Clifford's supposed claims on her and linking her with a man for whom she had no more than a friendly affection.

In fact, Bryden had tonight raised a further barrier, one even more insurmountable, for no man could have told her more definitely that he had no intention of marrying her, however much she might love him. Her heart ached with the pain of his blunt assertion, for she knew that he was warning her off. Perhaps he really did love Suzanne and was adopting what he believed to be a tactful way of telling Lexa that she hadn't the ghost of a chance.

CHAPTER FIVE

EDGAR had advised the two girls that an early start was arranged for the next day and they must not dally.

'Sometimes it is worse than being at school,' complained Gabrielle, as she finished packing her canvas bag. 'Timetables everywhere, even for pleasure.'

'Probably he doesn't want us to miss one of the best parts of the day,' answered Lexa soothingly.

'Early morning is not *my* best part of the day. Nighttime is more romantic.' As they walked out of the inn, Gabrielle gave her companion a mischievous glance. 'Was that how you found it last night?'

'Found what?'

Gabrielle's young laughter echoed across the courtyard. 'One can never believe that the English ever let themselves fall in love. So matter-of-fact, so sedate. Now, if Stefano had been here last night——'

But Edgar was taking their luggage and stowing it in the car, so Lexa was glad of the sudden end to this dangerous conversation. Surely Gabrielle did not suspect——? Lexa must try to be less transparent, however difficult that might be.

The morning's run was to Corte, an old town clinging to a peak rising abruptly from a bare plateau. The fortress commanded an extensive view of the surrounding territory and must have been almost impregnable as a defence when the town was threatened. Narrow streets of ancient houses clustered around the church with its tall domed tower and Lexa and Gabrielle had time to spend half an hour wandering through the market place, before meeting Bryden and Edgar again outside one of the principal hotels.

'No lunch?' queried Gabrielle in dismay, as Edgar held the car door open for her. 'I thought we were stopping here for——'

'Slimming day today,' returned Edgar smugly. 'Do you good.'

'The girl thinks of nothing but food,' muttered Bryden as he resumed the driving seat. 'Are you the same, Lexa?' he asked over his shoulder.

'I do occasionally have other thoughts in my head, but that depends on how hungry I am at the time.'

After a few minutes Bryden stopped at the edge of the town outside a fairly small inn which appeared to be entirely shut.

'You're out of luck, perhaps, Bryden,' Gabrielle jeered, as he rapped at the heavy wooden door.

But the sound of bolts being drawn back indicated that the place was not deserted and a few moments later the party of four were being shown into a small room, where the table was already laid for lunch.

'This little inn is usually open only in the holiday season,' Bryden explained to Lexa, as they arranged their places at the table. 'But this year we've had some alterations done and it's taken rather longer than we expected, so the place won't be open to visitors for another fortnight or so.'

As always, the food was delightful, including a dish of wild boar cooked with wine and chestnut sauce, followed by an omelette made of *brocciu*, a fresh white cheese and flavoured with mint.

Even Gabrielle pronounced herself satisfied at the end of the last course. 'I think I may last out now until dinner time,' she said with a sly glance at Bryden.

When the two girls left the inn, Lexa noticed Bryden standing by the car and apparently in conversation with a man in an aggressive attitude.

'Gregorio Moriani?' Lexa asked Gabrielle.

'Yes. He often makes himself a nuisance to Bryden and Edgar.'

'I've met him only once, but he's easily recognisable. He's exactly like a bandit.'

Gregorio was shaking his fist almost under Bryden's nose and Lexa wondered apprehensively if the Corsican was spoiling for a fight. Edgar appeared then and motioned to Lexa and Gabrielle to enter the car. Finally Bryden opened his door and shouted a parting shot to Gregorio. 'Why don't you get your lazy son to do a day's work sometimes?' He spoke in French, but Gregorio's retort was in the dialect which Lexa could not understand.

Gabrielle giggled. 'Such language! Not fit for Lexa's English ears!'

'What did he say?' Lexa was curious to know.

'That Bryden had a toad for a mother and that he is no better than a beetle that should be crushed under the foot.'

'Moriani is annoyed because he owns that other place opposite,' explained Edgar. 'We bought this rather ramshackle rival place, extended it, smartened it up enough to be comfortable, and Moriani knows that he's going to lose what little trade he had for his shabby inn.'

Bryden drove back to the centre of Corte where the party were to stay the night.

'Edgar and I are going out to one or two of the mountain villages this afternoon,' Bryden told Lexa when they were standing in the entrance hall of the hotel. 'If you'd like to come, you'd see another aspect of the island.'

'I'd like that very much.' She saw no reason to hesitate or refuse, since Edgar would be with her and Bryden, even if Gabrielle did not want to take the excursion.

Half an hour later she was ready and waiting when Edgar said, 'You and Bryden can go off to these villages. I have a couple of friends here in Corte whom I'd like to visit.'

'And Gabrielle?' Lexa queried, torn between apprehension at being alone with Bryden and exultation at the same prospect.

'Oh, she may decide to come with me or potter around the shops.'

Lexa accepted this unexpected journey as a gift from

Providence and hoped that Bryden would not feel that an unnecessary passenger had been forced on him.

In the car he said nothing about the altered arrangement, but gave her a large-scale map of the island.

'You'll see that I'm going out to two small villages, Sermano and Bustanico, but I have to come back to the main road that goes to Ponte Leccia before I can turn off for the other places.'

She was so delighted to be in his company that she would hardly have cared if he had said he intended to drive right over the tops of the mountains and slither down the other side.

'Do you own inns at all these places in the mountains?' she asked as he took a left fork that climbed up towards the peaks.

'Not yet!' he answered with a laugh. 'One has to go cautiously when you want to buy and not show too much interest. We have a couple in this ring of villages between Corte and the coast and I'd like to acquire several more, particularly the small inns, so that we can keep them still with their own character, but perhaps more modernised inside, wash-basins, baths—mod. cons. like that. These mountain villages can be so hideously ruined by the wrong kind of development. All we want to do is encourage a few more tourists to come to the interior of the island, instead of always hugging the coastal resorts. But they must be the right people and not expect huge hotels with casinos. If we go slowly, we'll build up a chain of small inns that offer comfort and good food and every facility for enjoying mountains and rivers.'

When he spoke of his plans for the future, Bryden sounded as though he had chosen Corsica's development as his life's ambition. Yet Lexa could not visualise that he would be content to remain here for the rest of his working life. Since, she told herself firmly, his whole future did not concern her, there was no need for her to worry over it.

At Sermano he stopped for a few minutes, although he said he had no property or business interests here.

'They say that the best singers in the whole island come

93

from this village,' he told her, as they walked towards the cemetery chapel of San Nicolao where there were some attractive frescoes.

It was here as she accompanied Bryden that Lexa had a sudden foreboding, some warning of an unknown danger. She dismissed the impression as swiftly as it had come. It was nothing but the contrast in temperature here in the chapel with the warmth outside; the atmosphere seemed chilly and without obviously hurrying, she was glad to leave. When she felt the warm sun on her neck and arms, she was ready to laugh at her fears. What possible harm could come to her in the company of Bryden? Now if her companion had been Philippe, she might perhaps have suspected some hidden purpose in taking her to these remote villages.

At the next village, Bustanico, Bryden had some arrangements to make with the innkeeper. 'I shan't be long, I expect. But you might like to look at a wooden crucifix made by a local man. It's just across the road there and round that corner. Don't lose yourself.'

The crucifix was handsomely painted and carved and Lexa stood there for some minutes in admiration, until she began to notice that several villagers were giving her curious glances. She wondered what was wrong with her. Was it her short, sleeveless dress of lilac cotton? Or that she was hatless?

She decided to return to the safety of Bryden's car which he had left unlocked for her benefit. When he rejoined her, she told him of the villagers' stares. He laughed.

'You're so obviously a foreigner that they wonder where you've come from.'

The road looped through the mountains back to the outskirts of Corte, then Bryden was driving north towards Ponte Leccia, but after some miles he turned off right along a narrow road with an unguarded slope down one side and the ground rising steeply on the other.

'If you look at the map, you'll see how the mountains force us to make huge detours. When we arrive first at San Pietro, then Calveroso, you'll find that there's little distance between them and the other two we visited earlier. Only the mountains in between.'

Lexa studied the map. 'No road, apparently.'

'Not for cars. Mules or donkeys or one's own feet. Shepherds have their own tracks, of course, but not much use to us.'

'Perhaps some day there'll be a connecting road,' she suggested.

'Doubtful. Corsica already has a respectable network of main roads. I'm not sure that I want too much easy communication. People who want to come to these attractive mountain villages must be prepared to take a little trouble to find them. Easy access ruins many beautiful places.'

At San Pietro, a small village with an inn of no more than four rooms, Bryden took Lexa inside with him. 'It's apparently not safe to leave you roaming around in these places,' he teased her.

His business dealings with the innkeeper were prolonged and produced much apparently heated conversation in French on Bryden's part and the Corsican dialect on the other. Eventually, matters were settled, no money changed hands, but wine was handed to Lexa and on leaving, she was given an enormous bunch of cherries, arranged and twisted together so that they resembled a bunch of grapes.

Bryden had to drive back to the fork in the road before he could take the other prong to Calveroso.

'I'm trying to buy the inn at this next village. It's not a bad little place, but neglected even more than the one we've just left, which incidentally, belongs to Gregorio Moriani.'

'But you were trading with the innkeeper there.'

He chuckled. 'Trading with the enemy? That man at San Pietro gets a better deal from me than he could hope to from Moriani, so he barters his goods with me.'

'I don't wonder that Gregorio doesn't have a good word for you,' she said. 'You undercut him everywhere and so he loses all his trade.'

'There's plenty left for him if he made fairer deals with the inn people and the shopkeepers. He's been cheating them for too long and they're ready to gain a little more profit for themselves.'

They drove along a narrow, winding road and came to Calveroso, a cluster of only a few houses fastened, it seemed, to the precipitous mountain slopes by the church tower.

The inn was not only shabby, but seemed deserted. Eventually a woman came from around the side and beckoned to Bryden, who followed her. This time Lexa stayed in the car, as Bryden had not invited her to accompany him.

She was content to wait, helped herself to a few cherries and gave herself up to pleasant thoughts, chiefly that this invitation to spend the afternoon with Bryden on a mountain tour would be a memory to cherish, even though he might have expected his father to accompany him.

The light was fading and the distant peaks glowed with pink and gold. Bryden was a long time transacting his business, but he had told her that he was negotiating for the purchase of the place, so that was probably why the haggling was protracted.

It was almost dark when he came out of the inn accompanied by the woman who was holding a lantern.

'I'm sorry I've kept you waiting so long,' he apologised as he seated himself in the car. 'The old man is ill and irritable and his wife is anxious to drive a hard bargain.'

'Have you settled about buying it?' she asked.

'Almost, I think, but they insist on time to think over my offer, which I think is reasonable, considering how run-down the place is.'

'They're not taking visitors?'

'Heavens, no. They haven't a room fit for a tourist to sleep in. They're open in the daytime to serve wine and a little food, but that's all. If we buy it, we shall have to spend plenty of money making it habitable, but it's in a good position.'

He was driving not too fast along the twisting road, then suddenly he jammed his brakes on as he turned a blind corner and then hit some obstacle that sent him and

Lexa jerking forward, almost through the windscreen.

Bryden was out of the car in a flash and she followed as soon as she had recovered her breath.

'What happened?' she asked, but no answer was necessary, for completely across the narrow road was a lorry laden with tree trunks. The driver's cab was hard up against the sloping mountain, the back wheels perilously near the drop on the other side and the long tree trunks overhung the back of the lorry in such a way that a slight touch might send the whole load crashing down the precipice by its own weight.

'No warning, no light, of course!' muttered Bryden angrily. 'A more efficient road block would be hard to imagine.'

He turned to examine his own car for possible damage. 'Lucky it's only the fender and a bent radiator.'

'What about the driver?' she asked.

He sighed. 'Yes, I ought to find out if the man is injured. There's a torch in my car. Get it for me, will you?'

She obeyed and then watched nervously as Bryden clambered up to the lorry's cab and peered inside. 'No one there,' he reported.

'He might be huddled up on the floor or even have fallen out on the ground the other side.'

'Yes,' agreed Bryden. 'That's a problem. I'm not sure how I can get round the other side to look. Unless—er— I might be able to see if I can get into the cab and lean out, but the door that side is jammed into the rock. I doubt if I can open it.'

Lexa was almost petrified with fright lest Bryden's movements should upset the precarious balance of the lorry and send it—and him—crashing down into the valley below.

'Be careful,' she implored.

After a few moments he rejoined her. 'No injured man there as far as I can see.'

'Where do you think the driver has gone, then?'

'Home, if he's sensible. Probably walked to one of the villages to get help. In the meantime, he leaves the most dangerous obstacle stuck clean across the road. No lights, no warning, of course.'

'I don't suppose he did it deliberately. Perhaps his brakes failed.'

'Then it's just as well that my brakes didn't,' he snapped. 'Otherwise we'd both be over the edge or flung about on the roadside.'

He walked towards the rear of the lorry and examined in the light of his torch the position of the back wheels.

When he came back, he took Lexa's arm and guided her back to the car. 'Let's sit inside and talk about what's to be done. I'm sorry I've landed you like this, but——'

'It's not your fault,' she said quickly.

'Not exactly, I know. But I ought to have left Calveroso sooner. Then we'd probably have avoided meeting this road block. I'd intended to suggest that we might get as far as Ponte Leccia and have dinner there, before we did the last stretch back to Corte, but I'm afraid that's out of the question now.'

'What do we do, then?' Her voice trembled a little, for panic was overtaking her. She was here alone with Bryden in the remote mountains and completely uncertain of his reactions.

'It might be possible for us to climb over the lorry and the tree trunks and drop down the other side, but even that wouldn't be very useful. We can't hoist the car with us over the other side.'

'Is it far to walk to—somewhere—and perhaps telephone for a car?'

'Impossible. The nearest habitation would be in the village of San Pietro where we went this evening, and it's a long walk.'

'If we met a car, we could give them a message, or they could pick us up.'

Bryden began to laugh. 'Few people are driving about in cars on these mountains at night. In the daytime, it's dicey enough.' After a long pause, he said heavily, 'I'm afraid, Lexa, there's nothing for it but to go back to that derelict place at Calveroso. They can probably find us some food. And, I trust, a bed for the night.'

She made no reply, her mind busy with the implications of the situation. She was remembering his earlier remarks, that the inn had no room fit for a tourist to sleep in. What exactly did that mean? That there were rooms in a dilapidated condition?

What sort of relationships had Bryden maintained with the various women in his past? What sort of reputation had he? She realised how little she really knew of this man with whom she had allowed herself to fall in love. All she knew was that two of his affairs—or romances—had ended disastrously. What of others?

'I shall have to back the car until I have room to turn.' His voice aroused her from her uncomfortable musings. 'Take the torch and guide me so that I don't go over the edge.'

She alighted from the car, but before closing the door, could not prevent herself from saying, 'And I suppose it doesn't matter if *I* fall over the edge.'

'If all you can do is make unhelpful remarks, I shall drive the car back myself and leave you to spend the night in any way you choose. You're welcome to climb into the driver's cab of the lorry—but the chances are that some clumsiness on your part will send the whole vehicle toppling down into the rocks below.'

'All right,' muttered Lexa. 'I know when I'm beaten.'

'Then use the torch properly and don't blind me.' He began to move slowly backwards, while she shone the torch downwards along the edge of the road both for his guidance and her own safety as she walked in its beam.

Up here the air was chilly and the wind blew through her thin dress. She had a jacket in the back of the car but she did not dare to disturb Bryden's concentration on reversing. It seemed hours that she walked along the precipitous margin avoiding the tufts of rough grass, several times making false steps when she failed to recognise the difference between some dark piece of vegetation and the shadowed gap in the cliff edge.

At last Bryden called to her that he thought the road was wide enough for him to turn. 'Just stand there and show me the edge.'

Twice her heart was in her mouth as he inched forward perilously, then twisted his front wheels just in time to avoid disaster. Then, 'That's it, I think,' he said with a relieved sigh. 'Get in.'

That was even easier said than done, for the door her side would open only halfway without hitting the rock face, but she managed to squeeze herself in. If she had expected a word of praise for her help, she was disappointed, for he drove off in silence.

Only one or two lights showed in the houses at Calveroso and the inn was in total darkness.

'Wait in the car while I find out what I can arrange,' he told her.

'Is it possible to telephone Edgar and let him know we're held up?'

'They've no phone here, but I'll do something about that later from another house.'

Lexa tried to make her mind a blank and let events overtake her without a hysterical approach.

It seemed ages before Bryden returned to the car, but she knew that no more than a quarter of an hour could have elapsed.

'They can provide food and fix us up with a bed. It will all be rather rough, anything but luxury, but at least we don't have to sleep out under the stars.'

Lexa shivered as she reached for her jacket and handbag. She had noted Bryden's repeated reference to 'a bed for the night'. Now he spoke of their having avoided sleeping 'under the stars'. She was uncertain of how much trust she could place in him, but by now she was strongly aware of how litle trust she could place in herself.

The room to which he now conducted her in the inn was small but tidy. A table covered with a checked brown and white cloth stood in the centre and held a large oil lamp. Several chairs of simple island design were set near the table and the floor seemed to be of bare wood.

The woman whom Lexa had seen on Bryden's first visit came in, cast a sharp glance at the girl, but smiled when

Bryden spoke to her in dialect, evidently introducing Lexa.

'This is the innkeeper's wife, Lexa,' he continued. 'Her name is Rosina.'

Lexa waited until the table had been laid with rough cutlery, stone mugs and a beautifully plaited straw basket for bread. Then she turned to Bryden. 'Could we see the rooms where we shall sleep?'

He smiled and there was a gleam in his eye that not only disconcerted her, but thoroughly alarmed her, so that her heart hammered wildly.

'Let's eat first,' he suggested, and his voice was deceptively gentle. 'We're both hungry and after a meal the poverty of the room won't strike you so badly.'

There it was again! *The* room. One room, not plural.

'I haven't much appetite,' she pleaded.

'If you've any sense at all in that frivolous head of yours, you'll eat what's put before you—and be thankful.' His gentleness had vanished, but she could cope better with his harshness than the soft, indulgent manner which seemed designed to allay any fears she might have.

When a bowl of steaming soup was set before her, Lexa knew that Bryden's advice was sound. Made of dried broad beans and cabbage spiced with ham, the soup was almost solid and a meal in itself, but it was followed by a meat dish unfamiliar to Lexa, but appetising all the same. By now she knew better than to offend Corsicans by refusing their homely cooking. A large flask of red wine accompanied the supper and Bryden generously filled Lexa's stone mug more than once.

'Not too much wine, please, Bryden,' she chided him towards the end, 'or I shan't know what I'm doing.' Even that phrase was not what she had meant to say and she was annoyed with herself when he immediately took up the opening.

'And not to be in strict charge of yourself would be a calamity?'

'Lack of self-control can always lead to a calamity,' she answered as smoothly as she could, but looking up, she caught the teasing gleam in his eyes. He was playing a cat-

and-mouse game, but she would refuse to be caught.

Her anxiety to see the room where she was to sleep had now given way to delaying tactics. The longer she dallied perhaps the better.

But Bryden easily saw through that ruse. Eventually he rose. 'Come along, Lexa, you're probably very tired after all the excitements of the evening. You'll want to go to bed. Rosina has probably arranged—everything—by now.'

She stood up reluctantly. 'Arranged—everything' sounded ominous.

'By the way, you were very good when I had to back the car along that mountain road. Many girls would have pan-icked or lost their heads, but you were all right and I'm glad I didn't have a hysterical girl on my hands as well as a tricky job to turn the car.'

It was the nearest he had ever come to giving her a compliment and even now, she could hardly believe his sincerity. It was part of the softening-up process.

The innkeeper's wife led the way upstairs to a small bed-room where a double bed, two chairs and a cupboard were the sole furnishings.

Rosina put the candle on the mantelpiece, said some-thing in dialect to Bryden and with a broad grin left the couple.

'What did she say?' demanded Lexa.

'That she hoped we would have a pleasant night.' Bryden was smiling in a way that made her long to slap his face.

'Pleasant—for whom?' She stood holding the brass knob at the foot of the bed, rigid, icy with apprehension, yet knowing that surrender would be sweet. Yet the circum-stances were all wrong. Attainment of desire should not happen casually like this, in sordid surroundings.

'Pleasant—for both of us, she meant.'

'Did you tell her that we were married?'

'Certainly not. There was no need for that. We are apparently spending the night together under the same roof and in Corsica that means that we should in due course be married. Honour demands it!'

Exultation rose within her, but she swiftly quelled it.

Bryden was English and so was she, and Corsican laws did not apply.

'Are you trying to test me?' She was now furiously angry more with herself than with him. 'Trying to see if I'm the girl who gives herself to any man who crooks his little finger at her?'

'I've no intention of crooking any of my fingers at you.'

'You knew about that road being blocked by the lorry,' she accused hotly.

'Rubbish! How could I know?'

She shrugged her shoulders. 'Villages have their own grapevines and news travels fast. That woman—Rosina—could have told you when you were here the first time.'

'And if she had, do you think I'd have been fool enough to risk going down there in the dark. I shouldn't have given myself the trouble, but stayed here.'

She hesitated before speaking again. 'Then if we have to stay here, you'd better find yourself some other room.'

'This is the only one available. I told you that the inn-keeper, Rosina's husband, is ill. We can hardly turn him out of his bed for the sake of your scruples.'

'Scruples! This sort of thing may be a common habit with you, but I assure you that——'

'You seem to be protesting too much! Has "this sort of thing" happened to you before? Is that what you're trying to tell me?'

'No, it isn't. And I've never been in this position until now.' She was near to tears, but she willed herself not to cry, for that would give him the chance to boast that he was not to be influenced by a woman's tears.

He took a step towards her and his eyes were gleaming with triumph. 'I don't try to take other men's girls,' he said slowly, his gaze fixed intently on her face. 'And you must have formed a very low opinion of me if you imagine that I would try to rape a girl who is a guest in my father's house. I could possibly have managed that without bringing you to a lonely inn in the mountains.'

She turned her head away. 'I'm sorry,' she muttered.

'Sorry, perhaps, that I'm not Philippe?' he taunted. 'Now

103

you might have enjoyed this little adventure with him as your partner.'

'No, never! But you might have liked Suzanne better as your companion.' She flung the words at him, but was amazed at his reaction, for he grasped her shoulders and shook her so violently that her head swung backwards and forwards like that of a rag doll. His fingers dug into her flesh until she wanted to cry out.

'You damn little fool! Can't you think of anything but cheap gibes?'

'You've given me a good example!'

He held her firmly by the shoulders, pinning her arms down to her sides, then he bent and kissed her mouth. At first her lips remained firmly passive, but then trembled as she gave up resisting. Her arms crept round his neck as she responded to the ardent pressure of his kiss. He crushed her in a fierce embrace that was rapture that she had never thought to experience, and although her mind warned her not to yield, her senses decided otherwise as she clung to him.

Then he relaxed his hold. 'That was a goodnight kiss to remember,' he said mildly. 'And you can go back to Clifford and tell him that you're as pure and untouched as when he left you here—and I hope he appreciates it.'

He walked swiftly out of the room before she had completely recovered her balance.

Now the full horror dawned on her. In that weak moment she had revealed unmistakably to him that he was the man she wanted.

She flung herself on the bed and now the tears streamed down her face, hot, angry tears that would never relieve the aching bitterness of self-revulsion or the fact that she had betrayed her deepest feelings in the most sensual and wanton manner.

CHAPTER SIX

AFTER the night's turmoil, Lexa could hardly believe that she had slept at all, but the entrance of Rosina with coffee and rolls, and a large jug of hot water to wash with, awakened her to her unfamiliar surroundings.

'*Bonjour, mademoiselle!*'

Lexa was now sufficiently awake to notice the keen glance that Rosina bestowed on the bed with apparently only one occupant. The woman set down the breakfast tray and jug, went out of the room and returned a few moments later with a large shallow basin and towel.

She murmured a few words in dialect and Lexa understood that Rosina was apologising for the lack of amenities.

'*N'importe,*' Lexa replied with a smile, but she waited until she was alone again before clambering out of the bed. She did not want Rosina to see that she had removed only her dress and slept in her underwear.

She washed quickly and put on her crumpled lilac cotton dress from yesterday. She tidied her hair as best she could with a pocket comb and dabbed her face with powder in her compact. The coffee was strong and of good flavour and the rolls crisp. Lexa felt the need of fortifying herself before the grim moment of meeting Bryden face to face again this morning.

As soon as she had finished her breakfast she went downstairs. The front door of the inn stood open and outside the morning air was fresh and exhilarating. The mountain peaks were tipped with coral as the sun climbed; one side of the valley was shadowed in blue-violet, while the other sparkled with different shades of green.

Bryden was standing across the road by the side of some rough fencing opposite the inn. Lexa hesitated before approaching him, wary as to his attitude. He was wearing the same cream sweater and brown trousers as yesterday, of course, and as she went towards him she could not control that magic lift of the heart that so often assailed her when she saw him.

He turned as she came level with him. 'Good morning,' she said quietly. 'What time do you want to start?'

'Depends on how quickly they can clear the road. Several of the villagers went down earlier this morning to help.'

'And the driver? Was he hurt?'

'Not at all. He was apparently coming up here when his brakes failed and he started to go backwards round the curve. The only thing he could do was ram the lorry into the mountainside—where we found it. Then he walked down to San Pietro, where he lives.'

After a pause, she asked, 'Were you able to telephone your father and tell him where we were?'

'Yes, I did that last night.'

Lexa had expected him to be icy in his manner, but his eyes glowed almost affectionately at her as he spoke. She felt the hot colour flush into her cheeks and hoped he would assume that it was the freshness of the morning air that caused it.

'We shall be told when the road's clear enough for us to go down, so in the meantime we might as well stroll about and look at the village. You didn't see much of it last night.'

First he paused in front of the inn. 'It's almost a ruin, as you can see, but it has possibilities and I think the owner, Rosina's husband, will accept my offer. He can't run the place himself, his health is too bad, but with the money he'd receive from me for the sale, he and Rosina could have a small house in the village and live there in comfort.'

He moved away a few steps and pointed to the side of the building. 'What I'd intend to do is pull down that old outhouse affair and build a new wing on there—all bed-rooms. The middle part is sound enough, but needs re-storing and redecorating and so on.'

Lexa now realised that Bryden was making an effort to regain at least some of the casual basis of toleration, if not friendship, that had existed until last night, and she was only too relieved to follow his lead.

He continued to tell her of his development plans and

106

took her towards the back of the inn, from which the most magnificent view of mountains and valleys extended.

'You see, it's a good place for tourists who want to get away from it all—especially if they get marooned completely up here by a lorry stuck across the road.' He darted her a teasing glance. 'All they need is a comfortable bedroom, with bath or shower, and good food.'

'Are you more interested in these projects than you were at your own architect's job?' she asked, as they walked along the rough path to the centre of the village.

'I don't know. This is interesting because it's on a very small scale and brings quick results. You get a stonemason and a carpenter on the job and in a short time you have the finished article—and open with a big bang.'

'And what you did before was on a larger scale?'

'Hospitals and schools, factories, blocks of offices—that sort of thing.'

Outside what was evidently the chief shop two women stood talking, one carrying a shopping basket of vegetables and a loaf of bread sticking out of the top. The other held an assortment of baskets and boxes made of plaited wood in what Lexa now knew to be the traditional Corsican manner. When she saw Lexa's interest, the woman proffered her wares for inspection and was obviously naming prices. But Lexa could not understand the dialect speech and turned towards Bryden for translation.

'That one is ten francs, she says. This one, which is a copy of Bastia work, that's twelve, and this little one is only six francs.'

Lexa was charmed with them all, but suddenly realised that she had left her handbag in the inn and therefore had no money with her.

Hurriedly she gave the baskets back to the woman and began to walk away, with apologies.

Bryden said, 'What's the matter? Didn't you like them? They were very cheap—and as there are so few tourists up here at present, she probably hasn't done much trade.'

Lexa shook her head. 'It wasn't that. I haven't any money with me.'

Bryden laughed. 'Soon remedied.' He took her arm and that same familiar thrill shot through her. The woman, sensing a sale, was already hurrying towards Lexa.

'Choose the one you want,' ordered Bryden.

Although she really wanted the one that was Bastia type, she chose the smallest because it cost least. A square basket, with a lid, about six inches each way, it would serve to hold odds and ends.

'It's only a loan, remember,' she said severely to him as they walked away from the basket-seller. She had noticed that he gave the woman a ten-franc note and told her to keep the change. Well, Lexa would reimburse him exactly in due course.

He showed her a little house that was empty. 'This is the one that would suit Rosina and her husband. I can get it for them for a low price and I'll have it painted and done up the way they want.'

'That's very considerate of you,' she murmured. 'You don't just turn people out when you want their property?'

He stared first at her, then laughed as though she had made a most humorous joke. 'You haven't the first notion about Corsicans, have you? Every man here regards himself as an emperor. He'll never be seen doing menial or labouring work if he can help it. That sort of thing is for the French or Italians. As for money, the very idea is pooh-poohed. Few Corsicans want to amass riches. All they want to do is produce enough food for their own needs—by bartering their surpluses—and then spend the rest of their time enjoying themselves in their own individual ways.'

He and Lexa turned a corner by a small tavern and Bryden continued, 'They're not exactly indolent. They'll work hard for a limited time, what they consider is just and fair. After that——' he broke off with a laugh. 'When I want alterations and construction work done at the inns or the new pavilions. I usually have to employ French or Italian labourers. But the islanders are unusually honest. They rarely accept tips of any kind—too proud and independent, and they will never steal. Thieving is regarded as 'a mean vice that no self-respecting Corsican would stoop to.'

At the foot of the village street a stream splashed and tumbled over a rocky bed. A plank bridge gave access to the opposite side and Bryden stepped firmly on it. Lexa noticed how it bounced under his weight and was not enthusiastic about following him, but she was more afraid of displaying her nervousness than of falling into the shallow water.

He turned and held out his hand to her and fire ran in her veins as his fingers grasped hers. Oh, she wished she could control these wild surges whenever Bryden touched her!

Almost on cue as if he had known her present thoughts, he asked, 'Did you sleep well last night?'

She was not prepared for this sudden query and her face reddened at the thought of the insults she had flung at him last night. 'Yes, I did.'

He was smiling down at her. 'You shouldn't jump to conclusions.'

'No. I'm sorry,' she admitted. 'But did you find somewhere to sleep? You said there was only that one room.'

'Would it have mattered to you if I'd been forced to sleep out of doors or in some outhouse?'

'Yes. I wouldn't have wanted you to be uncomfortable.'

'Liar! In the mood you were in last night you'd have been only too pleased if I'd had to sleep in the courtyard on the ground with the snow falling around me.'

'Well, it's not that time of year for snow.'

'No, but it could have rained hard—enough to give me pneumonia.'

She was immensely grateful to him now for giving her the opportunity to put last night's incident into its proper perspective, even though she could not tell him that.

By the time Bryden had made a circular tour of the village and conducted her back across the stream by another bridge, more substantial this time, to the inn, the woman Rosina was waving and shouting that the road was clear now.

Lexa could not decide whether she would be glad or sorry

to remember the village of Calveroso. It would take a considerable time before she could reflect without shame on her own conduct and the easy way she had surrendered to Bryden's embrace, an embrace that he had clearly shown was not meant as a loving gesture, but one of fierce distaste.

The road down to Ponte Leccia was clear as far as the fork where half a dozen men stood chatting. Bryden slowed down and asked about the lorry. Lexa understood by the answers that the task had been satisfactorily completed.

'How would they avoid tipping the whole load down the precipice?' she asked, when Bryden was moving off again.

'They attach strong ropes to the tree trunks and pull as the driver eases the lorry backwards and forwards to get it clear of the mountainside.'

As soon as she arrived at the hotel in Corte, Lexa rushed up to her room, but Gabrielle had seen her come in and almost immediately entered.

'I'm most glad to see you, Lexa,' she said warmly. 'Was it comfortable where you had to stay?'

Lexa could have shouted that some of last night's apprehensive moments had been decidedly uncomfortable, but she schooled herself to answer casually, 'Oh, yes, it was all right. Simple, but clean.'

Gabrielle sat on Lexa's bed and began to giggle. 'I wish I could have been shut up in a little inn with my Stefano. Then, you see, we would have had to be engaged.'

'But neither of you are Corsicans,' pointed out Lexa, realising this was dangerous ground.

'No. True, but when in Rome—you know——'

'I must have a bath before lunch,' Lexa cut in. She stepped out of the creased lilac dress and wondered if she would ever wear it again. Perhaps she would do so deliberately sometimes in the future, to remind herself of the folly of responding to a man who had no love to give.

Edgar seemed to think that the whole incident was only of the slightest concern. 'It was fortunate that Bryden didn't crash into that lorry. Or that another vehicle didn't come behind and smash you into it. Most Corsican drivers imagine that they're taking part in rallies or racetrack events when they come down the hills.'

When the party left Corte next day, Lexa turned to glance back at the little town sheltering beneath the rocky citadel, the river Tavignano dividing the town and behind, the mauve peaks of Mount Rotondo.

'Aren't you glad to be living in such a lovely island?' Lexa inquired of Gabrielle as they sat together in the car.

'Ah, yes,' sighed Gabrielle. 'But it is not Paris.'

'I'm thankful it's a little quieter than Paris,' Edgar put in grimly. 'And take it to heart, my girl,' he leaned over from the front seat, 'unless you work really hard at your fiddle, you won't see Paris in the autumn.'

Gabrielle made a monkey face at her stepfather.

'If you want the most beautiful scenery of all the island, Lexa,' Bryden suddenly chipped in, 'we shall be coming to it later today. We must get to Porto by sunset.'

They stopped for lunch at Evisa, a little town surrounded by pines and chestnut forests and clinging precariously, it seemed, to the slope of a mountain overlooking wonderful vistas of the sea.

Bryden had a business call to make after lunch, but joined his father and the two girls later in the afternoon.

'You mustn't doze,' warned Edgar, 'or you'll miss the Gorges de la Spelunca.'

'I'm wide awake,' replied Lexa indignantly.

'Actually, I think the views are better if one is driving up the road from Porto,' Edgar added, 'but Bryden will not be persuaded to drive backwards, I fear.'

The views were breathtaking from any direction. Cone-shaped mountains, rosy-tinted at their summits, soared almost vertically from dense vegetation. Lexa uttered little gasps of admiration.

'Wait until we get to Porto,' Edgar told her, 'and you'll run out of praise.'

Lexa's high expectations were more than matched by the incomparable splendour of the Gulf of Porto cutting deeply into the coastline like a fjord, for the cliffs were of magnificent rose-red granite and completely magical in the sunset.

111

Eucalyptus trees grew right down to the edges of the sandy beaches at Porto and a watchtower stood sentinel on a promontory of red rocks.

'Is there time to go along to the Calanques?' Edgar asked his son.

'We might just catch the last of the sun if we hurry, unless, of course, you two girls are willing to get up at dawn and see the sunrise,' Bryden answered.

'No, sunset's the best time,' his father objected.

Bryden took the coast road towards Piana and soon the spectacular labyrinth of crimson cliffs came into view. Wind and sea together had carved the cliffs into fantastic shapes, twisted pyramids, grotesque animals, mythical monsters.

'But you must have visited these places with Clifford?' queried Gabrielle.

Lexa shook her head, remembering that Clifford had chosen more sophisticated resorts. It was not, she reflected in his defence, that he was insensitive to natural beauty, but he preferred to be surrounded by people.

For herself, even while she revelled in the breathtaking splendours of the island, Lexa was obsessed by the feeling that this short holiday with Edgar, Bryden and Gabrielle was destined to have a dramatic effect on future events.

The hotel where the four were to spend the night was evidently one of the best in Porto, for it was set along the wooded valley and commanded a superb view of the bay and beach below.

After dinner, Edgar suggested going along to a café where there would be dancing and possibly local singers to entertain visitors.

'Dancing with us pair of old familiars is going to be pretty tame for the two girls,' interposed Bryden, as he leaned against the balustrade of the terrace. 'There's usually a boat trip at night to Girolata. That might be a pleasant way of spending the rest of the evening.'

Lexa would have joyfully welcomed the chance of dancing with Bryden, but perhaps, she reflected quickly, it was because he was not eager to dance with her that he had now

112

suggested a different form of entertainment.

Down at the harbour the boat was loading up. It was small and would hold no more than twenty passengers. Lexa and the others hastened aboard before all the most comfortable places were taken, but she was careful to sit between Edgar and Gabrielle, so that there could be no suggestion that she had contrived a seat next to Bryden.

In any case, he had strolled away towards some friends and stayed chatting with them for some time. Lexa noticed that among them was a very pretty dark-haired girl wearing a coral-coloured dress with a white shawl around her shoulders. She was accompanied by two young men, but that apparently did not prevent her from holding what was apparently a lively conversation with Bryden, during the course of which she seemed to tease him, then clasp his arm in an appealing manner.

Lexa, as she watched, was shocked at the raging jealousy which tore at her, and eventually she wrenched her gaze from the sight and concentrated on the dark, rippling water of the bay, the shadowed cliffs that plunged down to the shore and the twinkling lights on the far side of the gulf.

The boat was illuminated by festoons of fairy lights and presently five men began a performance of traditional folk songs. Two guitars accompanied, but there was also a zither and a pipe.

'The guitar is only a fairly recent innovation,' explained Edgar, 'and nowadays you don't find many with zithers and very rarely a Jew's harp.'

Dreamily, Lexa listened to the songs, the laments of griefs and wars and violent deaths followed by gentler and more melodious airs.

'The island songs have been influenced by contact with Italy,' Edgar pointed out. 'Originally they were much harsher and indeed, if we can persuade this lot to sing us a *Paghiella*, you'll hear how rough and harsh it can be.'

When eventually the singers were persuaded by various passengers to sing in this style, an archaic form of three-part singing for male voices, Lexa had noticed that only verbal requests were successful. Several times money was offered, but courteously and firmly waved away. The group would sing if they chose, but not for tips.

Lexa was astonished at the type of song, although she could not understand the words, but the whole effect was both mystical and deeply stirring in a strange way.

'In some villages they sing the Mass in this way,' Bryden whispered to her. 'Usually on feast days.'

She had been aware for some time that he had returned from his group of friends and the girl in the coral dress had disappeared.

'Are these religious songs which they are singing now?' Lexa asked.

'No, but they are traditional and often belong to particular local places.'

With Bryden near her, she felt secure, for in the songs of this wild island there was something atavistic, some deep primeval urge that stripped off the veneer of orthodox behaviour. She wanted to get up and dance, seize Bryden in a mad embrace, regardless of onlookers or propriety. She gave a deep sigh when the song ended and was glad to relax with a glass of wine which Bryden was pouring for her. He had evidently purchased a bottle from the bar.

The boat did not land at Girolata, a small wooded bay defended by a fort which Bryden told her was Genoese.

'The Genoese were great ones for building forts all round the coast as a defence against pirates. Most of the Mediterranean was infested by pirates of one race or another and there was plenty to plunder here.'

'Do you know all the history of Corsica?'

Bryden laughed quietly. 'Am I boring you? You make me feel like a schoolmaster with an unwilling pupil staying in after school hours.'

'I didn't mean to,' she apologised.

'Then don't ask sarcastic questions. Corsica's history is one long turmoil from prehistoric times, then Greeks and Romans. In the Middle Ages, the Pisans and Genoese, until Genoa sold her rights on the island to France, so it became a French province, but there were still storms and rebellions.'

'I've been to Filitosa to see the menhirs that have been excavated. Extraordinary sculptures of warriors.'

Now the singers were crooning a lullaby for the homeward journey and Lexa was content to listen to Bryden relating history or keeping silent, for somehow Gabrielle had vacated her place which had been taken by Bryden. Occasionally as the boat changed course to avoid unseen rocks in the darkness, Lexa was gently pushed against this man next to her, the man whose merest touch sent her into an ecstasy of delight.

Next day Bryden drove along the coast road south to Tiuccia, a little village sheltering under a rock crowned by a ruined feudal castle. There were long stretches of sandy beaches and Gabrielle demanded a chance to bathe there before lunch.

'Then you'll have to put up with a snack lunch,' he said. 'I have to make a detour inland before I can join the road to Ajaccio.'

'O.K. Suits me,' she answered airily, 'as long as you or somebody else will go and shop for what we eat.'

Bryden gave her a resigned look. 'Spoilt brat! Never happy unless someone is waiting on you. Mark my words, Gaby, one day you'll be so fat that you'll have to roll like a tub instead of walking.'

Gabrielle gave a delighted laugh. It occurred to Lexa when she was in the clear, warm water swimming or floating alongside Gabrielle that she had never seen Bryden swimming.

'Doesn't he bathe or swim?' she queried.

'Of course. When he can find the time! He can do everything in the water, dive, swim underwater sometimes for fish. Bryden is very clever,' Gabrielle continued with a hint of pride. 'He's very good at climbing mountains. Once he went on a rescue search for two climbers lost in the mountains. He found them and brought them to safety when the others had given up hope.'

'You love Bryden as if he were your brother, don't you?' commented Lexa with affection.

'Oh, yes. He is really the brother I never had when I was

a child.' Gabrielle laughed happily as she turned on her back and observed the azure sky. 'I think if he were not my brother by marriage, as it were, I could fall in love with him and want to marry him. But of course, there is Stefano—and I'm very fond of him.'

'And Stefano isn't at all like Bryden, I gather.'

'No. But he has qualities. Come, Lexa, we must go back to the shore or my beloved brother will be screaming to murder me!'

It seemed that Edgar had done the shopping and bought food at a café, fruit from a stall, while Bryden contributed a couple of bottles of wine.

As she enjoyed this picnic meal on the sandy beach, Lexa regretted that this was the last day of a short holiday and that it was unlikely she would ever again be touring part of the island with Bryden. She was really here in Corsica to earn at least part of her keep. And Bryden? He had his own interests, and Lexa was not one of his important ones.

For the next few days Lexa and Gabrielle worked diligently at their musical studies. As Gabrielle remarked, 'A little holiday is most welcome when one has to slave day by day.'

'Slave?' Lexa's eyebrows rose.

'Yes, indeed, slave! Here I am with my fingers worn down to the bone, my arm aching and my chin getting double to hold the fiddle. Sometimes I wish I had chosen the cello. That sits on the floor on its spike and you don't have to hold it.'

But Gabrielle's grumbles were not intended to be taken seriously, as Lexa knew.

When Gabrielle went to her master class at Sartène and possibly to meet Stefano for a stolen half-hour or so, Edgar suggested that Lexa might like to watch the nature film for which he was composing the music.

She was delighted with the idea when she found that in his own studio he had set up a screen with a projector.

'You'll have to watch it several times,' he told her. 'The first time just imagine you're seeing it on television and don't bother about the sound. After that, we can run a

116

piece of film at a time and watch the movements.'

The film described the seasons of the year in the wild life sanctuary of Coto Doñana in the south of Spain.

'It's one of the most interesting nature spots of Europe,' Edgar told her, 'and some day I really must visit it.'

The film began with a general view of this unusual area of wilderness, part sand dune, part swampland and a great deal of water in the form of small lakes strung out like the beads of a rosary. Many oak trees stood alone, their gaunt branches ideal supports for birds' nests. There were also shrubs and tufts of grasses to provide havens for water birds.

The arrival of aquatic birds from northern countries in the autumn was a wonderful sight. Hundreds of coots and purple birds whom Lexa could not identify splashed about like children and then would take off with an obvious clattering of wings. There were kestrels hovering almost motionless over their possible prey, dancing egrets and nightjars flying with huge open mouths to trap insects.

The film progressed through autumn to winter, then spring, with all the seasonal changes, and at the end Lexa was enthusiastic, sensing the immense possibilities of matching the images to music.

'The method I've used before,' Edgar pointed out, 'is to work small isolated passages to synchronise with the birds' or animals' movements, and find which orchestral instruments turn out best. We can easily build the opening passages to suit the landscape, then knit the fragments together.'

This was entirely new territory to Lexa and she was eager to write down the suggested notes when Edgar ran the film a second time. As he tried them out on the piano, she scribbled them on the staves, and listened to his comments—'Bassoon there, I think, those three notes,' or 'Twiddly bits on the flute, followed by last note on drum.'

Even when Edgar suggested they should finish work for one day, her mind's eye was occupied with flashes of coots and ducks skidding to a stop as they braked on the water, or the grotesque griffon vultures lurching and rolling about

117

in their drunken manner. In imagination she could hear snatches of tunes that might or might not fit, but were still a delight to carry around with one.

Then into this felicitous frame of mind came a thunderclap, shattering Lexa's peace and happiness, it seemed, irrevocably.

Philippe and Suzanne called at Fontenay in the late afternoon when Lexa happened to be idling on the terrace before it was time to change for dinner.

'So you went up in the mountains for a few days,' Philippe greeted her. 'Why did you not tell me?'

Lexa regarded him calmly. 'Should I tell you my day-to-day movements? Surely they are not your concern.' She spoke coldly, but afterwards realised that was a mistake.

'But of course where you go is my concern, very much my concern,' he said quickly.

'It was arranged by Mr Frankland as a—well, as a kind of treat, a little holiday for Gabrielle and me. We had worked well, he said.'

'And Bryden? He was also entitled to the little holiday?' Philippe's dark eyes flashed with malice.

'He had business calls to make in some of the mountain villages.'

'I, too, sometimes have business calls in the mountains, and I shall be delighted to take you with me at any time,' he offered.

'Thank you, Philippe, but I'm not always available. I have to work part of the time.'

'Pouf! Work! You speak as though you were chained to an office desk or behind the counter of a shop. Your time is flexible.'

During this time Suzanne had been standing in a corner of the terrace, her back towards Lexa. Now she turned. 'Lexa, you said you wanted me to make you a dress. Shall we go to your bedroom where we can discuss what you would like? Philippe has already had his share of your company.'

Lexa was astounded. She had never asked Suzanne for help in dressmaking, although she had admired a dress that the other girl had made for herself.

'But, Suzanne, I—er—yes, all right.' Lexa had already understood the signal in Suzanne's eyes, which meant 'I want to talk to you in private.'

'You will excuse us, Philippe,' she now said as she turned to go indoors.

Suzanne waited until she reached Lexa's room. 'Please close the door. We shall not be disturbed?'

'What is it, Suzanne?' Lexa was a trifle impatient with this determined air of mystery on Suzanne's part. 'Why did you say I'd asked you to make me a dress? I've no material. I——'

'Please! That was only an excuse, for we must talk.' Lexa had already seated herself by the window, but Suzanne remained standing. Now she approached Lexa menacingly. 'So now Bryden will marry you!'

The words were slow to register with Lexa. 'Marry me? What are you talking about?'

'You stayed the night at an inn in the mountains. So of course he must marry you. He has no choice.'

When the full impact of Suzanne's train of thought reached her, Lexa began to laugh quietly. 'Really! How absurd to think that! Neither Bryden nor I are Corsicans, if that's what you mean. Your traditional ideas may be different, but there's no reason at all why Bryden would have to marry me. We didn't sleep in the same room.' Lexa was remembering with an uncomfortable pang that scene with Bryden.

Suzanne, in her turn, began to laugh, but without mirth. 'And who will believe that?'

'But who would *not*?' retorted Lexa. 'The matter was very simple. Bryden and I stayed a night in the same inn because the road was blocked. And,' as a sudden suspicion darted into her mind, 'how do you know where we stayed?'

'My father knows exactly. He always knows what goes on in the mountains.'

'Ah, yes, the grapevine. So he told you about Bryden and me. Don't you realise, Suzanne, that your father is so much against your marrying Bryden that he would tell you any discrediting tale to prevent it?'

Suzanne whirled around on Lexa. 'That's not true! My father cares very much about my future. At present, he doesn't understand how much I love Bryden, but when he does, he will then do all he can to make me happy.'

Lexa stared at the other girl. 'And does your selfish mind have any consideration for Bryden's happiness?'

'But naturally he will be happy with me.' Suzanne swung back her long blonde hair. 'You are jealous of me, Lexa. You are in love with him and that is why you tricked him at that inn. You imagined that he would marry you very soon, but it is plain that he is not to be won by your tricks. You are English and too cold. I am not only French, but also Corsican, partly, so I know how to love with passion and fire.'

'I don't know how you could suppose that either Bryden or I could have arranged a lorry blocking the road home. You accuse me of secretly planning that we should have to stay up there at the inn overnight, but you flatter me. I'm not as clever as that.'

'How does anyone know that there *was* a lorry?' Suzanne gave Lexa the sweetest of smiles.

'Don't be ridiculous! I saw it myself.'

'You *say* you saw it.'

'And next morning Bryden told me that some men had gone down with ropes to help shift it off the road.'

Suzanne remained smiling. 'Bryden *told* you? There is no proof.'

Lexa was fast losing patience. 'Then if your father knows everything that goes on in that part of the mountains, find out for yourself. Or will you not believe the truth when you're determined to accept a lie?'

Suzanne was pacing up and down the room and Lexa burst out, 'For heaven's sake stand still in one place or else sit down! Don't behave like a young caged animal.'

Suzanne's young face took on a malevolent expression and her dark brown eyes glittered angrily. 'You are most insulting! You don't like it when I have found you out and your schemes have not succeeded. But I have my plans and

I shall win.'

A cold shiver went through Lexa's frame. What mischief was Suzanne up to now?

'If you mean to win Bryden,' she said slowly, 'your present tactics are not much use, are they? He's been living here, as your neighbour, for quite a long time, but you don't seem to have made much impression on him.'

In spite of her inward fears, perhaps for Bryden more than for herself, Lexa was determined not to show lack of mettle.

'Everything was happy between Bryden and me until you came,' Suzanne retorted. 'In any case, *you* are most selfish, for you have your fiancé in England. Have you forgotten that young man so soon?'

So Clifford was to be used now as Lexa's alternative.

'Clifford is not my fiancé,' she said emphatically. 'We were never engaged and he's quite free.' After a pause during which she looked straight into Suzanne's eyes, she added, 'So am I. Entirely free.'

Suzanne stared in return. Then her face puckered and slow tears rolled down her cheeks. 'Oh, I wish so much that you could have fallen in love with my brother. Now what is wrong with Philippe? He would make you a good husband. Why can't you love him? That would make matters easy for everyone.'

'Unfortunately, life isn't like that,' snapped Lexa. 'I can't fall in love with Philippe because you order me to, so that we could make a very tidy foursome.'

'Then you admit that you love Bryden!' Suzanne pounced in triumph on that half admission by Lexa.

'I admit nothing!' Lexa felt her colour rising into her face. 'Do you think I stayed here in Corsica just to fall in love with Bryden? I shall leave here in the autumn and then—Bryden will be just a pleasant memory. The son of some good friends I stayed with on the island.' The traitorous words rushed out and she was appalled by her own mendacity. But better to deny her own love for Bryden than allow Suzanne to know for certain the real truth. The girl could only guess, and those guesses were coloured by her own jealousy.

It seemed that Suzanne's fiery rage had fizzled out. She jumped up from the chair into which she had flung herself a few moments ago. 'We must go downstairs. Philippe will be wanting to talk to you.'

Lexa did not answer. At present she wanted to avoid Philippe as much as possible. 'I have to change my dress,' she said. 'I'll be down in a few minutes.'

Under the shower, she felt that perhaps she was also cleansing herself of Suzanne's ignoble accusations, but her own honesty insisted that however strong her denials her longing for Bryden and the comforting feel of his arms about her was no less than Suzanne's plainly avowed intention of securing him.

She chose a smoky-blue dress of soft jersey and brushed her bronze hair into a shining mass with the ends curled under. She dallied over her renewed make-up and hoped that by the time dinner was ready, Philippe and Suzanne would have left. But when she went down, the pair were evidently staying, for they were on the terrace with Marguerite and Gabrielle. Edgar joined the party in a few minutes and helped himself to a Martini.

At dinner Bryden was not present and for once Lexa was glad of his absence. She did not want every slightest glance or casual remark to be seized on by Philippe or Suzanne and magnified into further accusations.

Gabrielle was unusually silent and apparently had her own problems. Lexa had no chance of asking questions until coffee was being served on the terrace.

'Stefano?' she whispered. 'Did you see him?'

'No,' Gabrielle answered morosely. 'He did not get my message last week, so he did not come to the café today and he is very angry with me.'

'Not necessarily,' assured Lexa. 'Perhaps business of some sort detained him.'

But Philippe had brought his coffee cup and sat down close to Lexa. 'I wish I had been the man,' he whispered. 'It would have made me very happy.'

'What would?' Lexa pretended not to follow his meaning.

122

'To have been your companion at the inn. I would have made you very happy, too.'

'Really?' She averted her face and edged her chair a little distance from him, but he interpreted that gesture as an invitation and he immediately moved nearer to her and grasped her hand.

Her thoughts were calm as she reflected how little his touch affected her, except the desire to be free. She wriggled her hand, but he intensified his grip and she remained still, for she realised that every form of rejection was a challenge to him.

'You must let me take you to the mountains—very soon,' he coaxed. 'One man shouldn't have all the luck.'

'I've no idea when I shall be free to go exploring,' she said in a louder voice.

'Then I shall kidnap you one day,' he warned, raising his own voice. The others looked across at him and Lexa, who rose swiftly to put her coffee cup on the tray near Marguerite.

For the rest of the time she avoided conversation with either Philippe or Suzanne by sitting between Marguerite and Edgar. When at last the pair went off in Philippe's rattling old car, she sighed with relief. Gabrielle and Edgar went indoors and Lexa was about to follow suit when Marguerite said slowly, 'I wish I could have more liking for Suzanne.'

Lexa was nonplussed. What could she say?

'She was disappointed that Bryden was not at home,' Marguerite continued. 'She makes her feelings so plain and clear. In one way, she's still a child, but sometimes, I think, a dangerous child.'

'You think she could harm Bryden?'

'I'm not sure. Bryden is not happy, but I would not like him to link his future with her for the sake of a very temporary happiness.'

Lexa shivered and was thankful that in the dim light of the corner lanterns on the terrace Marguerite could not see her.

'Bryden has had so much unhappiness in his life. A few

years ago he was engaged and about to be married to a very lovely girl. Only a week before the wedding she eloped with another man. Tragically she was killed in a plane accident—the man as well and the pilot, too. Bryden was overwhelmed with grief, not only for the girl, but because he considered she had been responsible for two other deaths.'

Lexa murmured, 'It must have been a sad time for him.'

'Then, several years later, he met another girl, they became engaged. I don't know what went wrong between them, but Bryden seemed reluctant to talk about the wedding or any plans. Perhaps he was uncertain—I don't know. But there was a party at someone's house and all the young people went swimming in the pool. The girl was drowned. So perhaps you can see that he feels he has no luck with girls.'

'Yes, I do see,' Lexa said quietly.

Marguerite sighed. 'I go on hoping that some day he'll find the right girl. I'm so very fond of him. I never had a son, but if I had, I would have wanted him to be like Bryden.'

Lexa understood the strong bond of affection that existed between Marguerite and her stepson.

Edgar's voice came from inside the house calling 'Marguerite! Are you ready to come in?'

The older woman rose. 'Yes, we must go in. Come, Lexa.'

Much later when Lexa was in bed and the sweet scents of the garden bushes and flowers floated up to her balcony windows, she wondered if Marguerite's revelations had been intended as an indirect recommendation that she, Lexa, would be more suitable as Bryden's wife than would Suzanne.

She shook herself impatiently. Why tangle with wild dreams and wishful thinking? After two tragedies, naturally Bryden would not be over-eager to link himself with any girl and Lexa dared not hope for the impossible, although now, after Suzanne's outburst, followed by Marguerite's disclosures, Lexa had never ached so much with longing for him. But she must steel herself against such wild desires and cease to fret because they would not be gratified.

CHAPTER SEVEN

WHEN Gabrielle went to her next master class in Sartène, she tried to persuade Lexa to accompany her.

'But I work for Edgar on Fridays,' Lexa objected. 'Either I copy out his scores or put in some time on the film music he's doing.'

'It's very important that you should come this week,' Gabrielle insisted. 'In any case Edgar will be driving me to Sartène, so you could also come.'

'What's your real reason? Stefano?'

Gabrielle nodded with a shamefaced smile. 'If you could meet him, you could explain——'

'Gabrielle dear, if I meet Stefano, I shall tell him the truth, that you have your career to think about and that your stepfather thinks you're too young to go in for serious attachments.'

'Then you'll come?' Gabrielle was not in the least dismayed. 'You can do your shopping in Sartène.'

Edgar drove the two girls into the town, promising to return at six o'clock for the return journey.

'Stefano will come to the café I told you about at four o'clock,' Gabrielle said to Lexa in parting.

The girl went off to the music rooms and Lexa returned to the main streets of the town, where old houses were built into the solid rock. She idled in the shops, bought an attractive necklace made of nuts and small shells, then found a café with tables outside where she could have an early lunch.

She had only just ordered when a voice shouted excitedly, 'Lexa!' Suzanne stood by the table, smiling in the most amiable manner. 'A most pleasant surprise. Do you come to Sartène every week?'

'No. Just when it happens to fit in with the others in the family.' Lexa did not intend to mention the object of today's visit.

'Me, I come most Fridays.'

'Will you join me for lunch?' invited Lexa, and Suzanne eagerly accepted.

When they were halfway through the meal Suzanne said, 'You must buy a dress length and let me make it up for you. I shall be most pleased to do this for you.'

Lexa was perplexed. If Suzanne was trying to apologise for her angry behaviour of a few days ago, then it would be gracious to accept such a token, but Lexa was unwilling to accept favours as well.

'All right,' she agreed, recognising Suzanne's skill, 'but you must let me pay you for the making.'

'Not at all! It will be entirely my pleasure. Besides, you have given me a very good lunch.'

Lexa hesitated to argue over the trifling matter. No doubt she could make some other recompense to Suzanne at a later date.

Suzanne declared that she knew of several good shops for dress material and after leaving the café conducted Lexa to a small shop that seemed little more than a doorway set between two larger buildings. A showcase held only three lengths of material, but Suzanne led the way upstairs to a large, well-lit room where rolls of cottons and synthetics, plain and patterned, were stacked on shelves up to the ceiling.

'You like a long dress for evenings?' Suzanne queried, measuring Lexa's height in a glance, pursing her lips. She then suggested, 'Green is your colour, but also chestnut browns and light yellows, with your hair and eyes.'

Lexa began to be appalled at the enormous number of materials spread out on a counter for her approval, but the assistant seemed not to mind. Eventually she chose, with Suzanne's approval, a very lovely fabric of bronze leaves on a cream background, with splashes of pale green and flame to give it vividness.

'Now,' said Suzanne, 'if you will let me take your measurements, I will take home the fabric, then cut it for you and you can then come to my home and be fitted.'

Lexa acquiesced in this arrangement, although she was not too keen to visit the house in case Philippe was there

126

and immediately interpreted her call in his own favour.

Now she took an occasional glance at the time and wondered how she could leave Suzanne for that appointment with the unknown Stefano. Eventually Suzanne herself solved that difficulty.

'At four o'clock I have to meet my father in the Square. If I am late he will probably beat me, so I must go!' she added, laughing.

'And I have to meet Gabrielle.'

'If I'd known you would be here in Sartène, I'd have told Philippe,' said Suzanne. 'He will be desolated to have missed you.'

'Give him my sympathy,' replied Lexa lightly. '*Au revoir.*'

Lexa was within a few yards of the Café Yolanda where she was to meet Stefano, when she saw Bryden on the opposite side of the street. Swiftly she averted her head and walked towards the café, but he had evidently seen her and dashed across the road.

'Hullo!' he greeted her.

'Oh! I didn't know you were here,' she replied, calling herself several kinds of fraud, for she would gladly have rushed across to greet him.

'My father telephoned me to pick you and Gabrielle up and take you home. Said it would save him an unnecessary journey.'

'Yes, of course,' she said, at a loss as to how to handle this unexpected awkwardness.

'What time does Gabrielle leave her class? About five?'

'Usually, I think.'

'Then in that case we've time to sit outside a café and watch the world go by for a while.'

'Well,' she began, 'I—I—er—have some more shopping to do.' It was the only excuse she could think of and she was furiously angry with fates or Providence or whatever it was that was robbing her of this heavenly chance of sitting for half an hour or so with Bryden.

'All right,' he said. 'I'll sit here and wait for you, unless you're going to be about three hours.'

Of all places, he was choosing to sit at a table outside

the Yolanda. What could she do now? Stefano might not turn up at all and then she would have denied herself an exquisite pleasure for nothing.

She glanced at her watch. Five minutes past four. There was no one sitting outside except a very elderly man studying a newspaper. Was Stefano inside the café? Probably, since his meetings with Gabrielle were clandestine and she would not expose herself to the danger of being recognised by passers-by.

A further cause for alarm asserted itself in Lexa's mind. Gabrielle would come innocently and eagerly to her rendezvous at the Yolanda and be confronted with Bryden. That would be disastrous, for Bryden would not expect his young stepsister to be involved in secret meetings with an Italian hotel receptionist. Or was it possible that he knew of these meetings and had come there today deliberately to see the man for himself?

Lexa tried to peer inside the café, but since she did not yet know Stefano, she realised it would be hopeless to pick him out of half a dozen young men who might be there in the shadows.

Bryden took her arm to swing her out of the way of passers-by and his touch gave her such fiery ecstasy that she was tempted to throw all caution to the winds and agree to whatever he suggested. But loyalty to Gabrielle was of some importance and she could not abandon the girl to the risk of being discovered in what might be a quite harmless intrigue.

Lexa decided that she must grasp the nettle. She was searching for the right words when Bryden looked down at her with a grin that upset all her sober balance. 'Off you go, then, and do this shopping. I'll wait.'

She took a deep breath and then let the words tumble out untidily. 'Bryden, I—I have an appointment.'

In her quick upward glance she saw his eyes harden. 'Where?'

'Here. At this café.'

He smiled. 'Philippe?'

Before she could stop the words, she had said, 'No. Not

Philippe.' She realised instantly that it would have been much better to have allowed Bryden to believe that she was meeting Philippe.

'Oh?' His eyebrows rose. 'You really are quite a girl for attracting the men, aren't you? Rush to you like a magnet. I now begin to wonder how many rivals poor old Clifford had at home. Has, in fact. For no doubt when you go home you'll look up all your boy-friends and play them off against one another.'

She closed her eyes in pain. She might have known that he would jump to the obvious conclusion, even though he had not bothered to ask if it were a woman with whom she had the appointment.

'I must go,' she mumbled.

'Of course. You mustn't keep him waiting. So long, then. I'll be in the car park about six—unless of course you're staying the evening here and your friend will provide transport.'

With misery clutching at her heart, she watched him turn smartly on his heel and stride off down the street. Oh, why did it have to be today when she had a prior commitment? She would have given a great deal to have had the courage to run after him, tell him that no other appointment mattered if only she could be with him for an hour or two. But common sense and dignity prevented her making such a futile exhibition of herself. Bryden would only laugh, tease her about defaulting on yet another admirer and succeed in making her feel cheap.

She entered the Café Yolanda and sat down at a table as far from the entrance as possible. She wanted to hide in the shadows. A waiter came, took her order for coffee, then a dark young man was standing by the table.

'You are Mademoiselle Merton?' he asked in French. 'I am Stefano.'

'Please sit down,' she invited. He was undeniably handsome, with brilliant dark eyes and lean features. Too attractive to a sixteen-year-old girl.

'I speak English if you prefer,' he offered. 'My accent not good, but the words comprehensible—I hope,' he added with a charming smile.

He ordered a glass of cognac and as he sipped it, waited for Lexa to start the conversation. Now she had no real idea of what she was supposed to do, except possibly hold the fort, as it were, until Gabrielle came along, in case he might think that the French girl was letting him down again.

'I think I must tell you'—she avoided saying 'warn'— 'that Gabrielle is only just sixteen and is expected to make music her career.'

'Love and music go together,' he said in a warm, vibrating voice.

'Perhaps, but a little later on, when Gabrielle is firmly placed in the musical world.'

'Are you perhaps an English aunt come to tell me that I am to stop loving Gabrielle?' he queried.

She shook her head. 'Not at all. I'm here this afternoon —and against my will—only to reassure you that Gabrielle will be coming today, she hopes. I believe you did not get the message she intended for you a week or so ago.'

'It did not matter. I am here today.'

The phrase darted into Lexa's mind—'and gone tomorrow, I hope!' Suddenly as though a torch had been shone into this young man's being, she saw beneath the glamorous exterior of his good looks. He was shallow and vain, Gabrielle was just an easy conquest for him and it was likely that he imagined she was the daughter of wealthy parents, since they could afford an expensive musical education for her.

'Would it matter very much to you if you stopped seeing her?' She shot the question at him and intently regarded the expression on his face. He paused to light a cigarette.

'Naturally. I should be brokenhearted.'

'For how long? A week?'

He smiled at her, then glanced down at the cigarette twisting in his fingers. 'I think you do not understand love, mademoiselle, forgive me.'

'What makes you say that?' she queried sharply.

'Because you think it can be turned on or off—like a tap.'

130

'But do you think there's a future for Gabrielle—with you? Do you want to marry her? And could you keep her?'

He looked across the table at her, a calm smile on his face. 'Mademoiselle, these are important questions. Have you the right to ask me? You are not a sister? A relative?'

'No. Only someone who is very fond of Gabrielle. I don't want to see her spoil her life almost before it's begun, by a romance that might not have a happy ending.'

He leaned his elbows on the table and confronted Lexa. 'There is something about you that is very attractive. Usually I do not care for English girls, but you are different. You have a spark that is——'

'Don't let's change the subject,' she interrupted hastily. 'We were talking about Gabrielle, not me. Would it be possible for you—if not to stop seeing her—then to make your meetings less frequent? You could always say that you can't get the time off because of the holiday season and the visitors.'

But Lexa's eloquent questions remained unanswered, for Gabrielle appeared at that moment, her face radiant when she saw Stefano. 'Then you have now met Stefano and explained how it was I could not meet him last time?'

Lexa let that pass in the flurry of ordering more coffee and something to eat for Gabrielle, who declared that she was starving on account of the delay in leaving her class.

'Oh, I was worried,' she said now, 'in case you did not find Stefano or had gone to the wrong café.' She turned towards the young man. 'Then you, Stefano, would have had another wasted journey.'

'No journey is wasted if there is a possibility of seeing you, *ma chérie*. Also today I have had the honour of meeting your charming friend and the time passed quickly.'

Easy flattery, thought Lexa. He was experienced in the art and Gabrielle, in the first flush of growing up, was no match for him.

After about a quarter of an hour, Lexa rose, 'I have a couple of shops I want to go to. Will you excuse me?' Naturally, Gabrielle would want Stefano to herself without a third party, and surely, reflected Lexa, there could be no harm in leaving the girl here in a café.

'Don't forget,' she said to Gabrielle. 'Bryden will be in the car park at six o'clock.'

'Bryden? I thought Edgar was coming for us.'

'No. Edgar arranged with Bryden to pick us up.'

Outside in the street Lexa hurried away from the café, not particularly pleased with herself or her behaviour. She had lowered herself in Bryden's estimation, giving him the idea that she was eager to collect young men acquaintances wherever they could be found. She had done nothing in Gabrielle's interests except leave her alone in a café with a dubious young man.

Lexa idled the remaining time away by making small purchases in a bookshop and stationer's. It was no use arriving at the car park too soon, for if Bryden were already there, she would face further questions from him about her newest male acquaintance.

Just before six o'clock she hovered near the car park, trying to see if Gabrielle were already there. Then it occurred to Lexa that the French girl, cocooned in a dreamy state, might forget about time and its urgencies. She hurried back to the Café Yolanda and halfway there was relieved when Stefano and Gabrielle came sauntering along the street.

'We ought to hurry,' whispered Lexa to the other girl. 'You know how impatient Bryden gets if he's kept waiting.'

'He must learn,' replied Gabrielle calmly.

Lexa had supposed that Gabrielle would say her fare-wells to Stefano before arriving at the square, but he accompanied the two girls almost up to Bryden's car. Lexa was thankful that Bryden had not yet appeared, but her relief was premature. Bryden came striding across the square and, apart from a hole opening up in the ground, there was no way of making Stefano disappear.

Gabrielle was visibly startled at the appearance of her stepbrother. The two men eyed each other, with Stefano smiling genially and Bryden frowning.

'You must introduce me,' he suggested to Lexa.

'Of course,' she replied hurriedly. Gabrielle's eyes were

imploring Lexa not to disclose the truth. 'Stefano—and this is Bryden, Gabrielle's brother.' She realised that she was ignorant of Stefano's surname and tried to gloss it over by not mentioning Bryden's English surname.

The smile had vanished from Stefano's lips and there was a wary look in his eyes. He turned towards Lexa. 'I am enchanted to see you today,' he said in French, 'and shall look forward to our next meeting.' Then he bent and kissed Lexa on both cheeks, before giving Gabrielle a mere friendly nod and a handshake.

'Sorry I have to deprive you of such charming company,' Bryden said in a most unamiable tone. 'Goodnight.'

'Au revoir!' called Stefano, waving his hand in salute as he walked away across the square.

In the car on the homeward journey Gabrielle was silent, causing Lexa much uneasiness, for as yet she could not even mention the subject of Stefano.

Bryden waited until Gabrielle had alighted and as Lexa followed, he asked in the cool, casual tone, 'And where did you pick *him* up—if I may be allowed to ask?'

Lexa's mouth set in a firm line. This situation had now become a charade, yet how could she betray Gabrielle until the latter realised that her affection for Stefano was infatuation and not love, or until he had made it plain to her that the fleeting attraction was over and that he was more concerned with fresh conquests?

'Are you really concerned with who I *pick up?*' Lexa temporised, accenting those last two words.

He shrugged. 'No, I suppose I've no right to catechise you. All the same, I might warn you that he looks like a *gigolo*. Does he dance well?'

'We haven't progressed that far,' she muttered, moving away from the car and towards the house.

'Italians often miss out some of the conventional intermediate stages of an affair. But then, of course, you would know that. You've probably become quite experienced since you came here.'

Choking rage welled up in Lexa and she groped for words, not to explain calmly and discreetly the true situation, but angry words that would sear and scourge Bryden in the most lacerating way. 'Perhaps you could leave me to find my own friends and friendships without interference—and I'll leave you to *your* affairs.' She ran indoors before he could reply.

Lexa flung herself down in the armchair by the window of her bedroom. What a day! If she had known earlier that a single meeting with Gabrielle's boy-friend would cause so much distress and wretchedness, she would never have agreed to Gabrielle's suggestion. The mischief was done now, but Lexa was horrified that she had allowed herself to be provoked into saying those last harsh words to Bryden.

Yet the day's misery was not ended, for in a few minutes Gabrielle entered Lexa's room, her face tear-stained, her eyes red with crying.

'Oh, I am so unhappy!' she sobbed, flopping on to Lexa's bed. 'Stefano has turned away from me and now he is attracted to you.'

'Nonsense!' snapped Lexa, unwilling yet forced to bear this extra burden of Gabrielle's affliction. 'Don't you understand? When he saw Bryden and knew he was your brother, he was careful not to take too much notice of you. That was why he kissed me and only shook hands with you. He wanted Bryden to believe that I was Stefano's friend, not you.'

'But Stefano *is* attracted to you. He told me so,' declared Gabrielle.

Lexa went to the bed and leaned over Gabrielle's shaking figure. 'Then if he's so easily attracted to someone else, he isn't worth much, is he?' Lexa eagerly seized the chance of undermining Gabrielle's faith in her Italian friend.

'But you wouldn't take him from me?' Gabrielle sat up and dried her eyes. 'That would be most cruel.'

'Look, *chérie*, this isn't the time to talk now, you're too upset, but later—perhaps tonight or tomorrow, I'd like to——'

'I know! You want to give me advice. You want to make me stop seeing Stefano.' Gabrielle spoke hotly.

'Wouldn't that be best? What good can come of this—this friendship?' Lexa could not call it love, for she knew it was infatuation on one side and heartless philandering on the other.

'I don't know,' wailed Gabrielle.

'If you think he's swung towards me, I can assure you that I shan't encourage him at all. He isn't the kind of man I like. He hadn't the courage to declare to Bryden that he was *your* friend. Oh, no, he had to fob himself off as one of mine—and I wasn't in the least enthusiastic. Gabrielle dear, he's no use as a permanent attachment. He'll chuck you for the next pretty face that takes his eye at the hotel or anywhere else.'

'I can't think now,' muttered the other girl. 'I'm too unhappy.'

'It will pass,' consoled Lexa. 'We all think at sixteen that we've met the love of our life—but it goes.'

'Was it like that with you?'

'Oh, yes,' answered Lexa airily. 'I had a crush on a handsome young man and I can't even remember his name now.'

'And you're not really keen on Stefano?'

'Indeed, no. I've other problems to occupy me.' Lexa's words were carelessly spoken, but Gabrielle immediately seized on an inner meaning.

'Yes, of course. You'll go back to England and marry Clifford.'

Lexa was sharply aware of this wrong interpretation, but she could not correct it now and disclose to Gabrielle that she had a restless and unfortunate longing for Bryden, an unrequited torment that would never be alleviated.

During the weekend Lexa felt it necessary to put in some extra time working on Edgar's scores. In his studio she was away from the chance meetings with Bryden and that cold, assessing look in his eyes.

On Sunday afternoon Edgar came in to see what she was doing. 'I thought we agreed on Sundays off, at least,' he complained.

'Well, I wasn't here on Friday, so I thought I'd catch up. Would you like to glance through these pages?' She handed him the neatly written music sheets.

'Very good indeed,' he complimented her after thoughtful study. 'This trio—I wonder if we could put this on at a recital that Marguerite is trying to arrange in Ajaccio.'

'The three of us? At a public concert?'

'Yes. Marguerite thinks that for Gabrielle to play in trios makes it easier for her than giving violin solos with piano accompaniment.'

'Yes, that's probably so. But I haven't done much piano-playing in public—well, not concerts. Only very local affairs, sometimes concert party stuff for entertainment.'

Edgar smiled at her. 'You'll be all right. Recitals with the other two would give you confidence, too.'

When he had gone, with the injunction that she was not to work more than another half an hour, she sat idle for a few moments, reflecting on the changed life that Corsica had provided for her this summer. Mixing with the musical world had always appealed to her, but she had never dreamed of rising to the heights where she would be participating in the première of a new work by a well-known composer.

She resumed her task, realising that if the trio were to be performed soon, three copies of the score at least would be needed. Unless, of course, the fair copy could be photo-copied. Was that what Edgar usually did before the work was finally printed? If he wanted three handwritten copies, then she would have to work at some speed to have them ready for the practice sessions.

The door opened and someone came in. Without glancing up, she knew that the visitor was Bryden, but she would not give him the satisfaction of a greeting or even speak the first word.

'You're a glutton for work, aren't you?' he teased.

'If you like the work you're doing, it's no hardship to put in time to it.' She deliberately made her voice sound cold and distant, even though her heart was hammering so loudly that she imagined he must hear it.

She was sitting on the piano stool facing the keyboard, and at her right hand was a large sloping board that swivelled on its pedestal. Edgar used it when he was composing so that he had a firm surface to scribble on. Now Lexa swung the table so that it provided an obstacle between her and Bryden as he stood by the end of the piano.

She wrote in three more bars, knowing that he was scrutinising her.

'I'm sorry I twitted you over your handsome friend in Sartène,' he said. 'I ought to have realised that———'

'No need to apologise. I've come to expect that kind of remark from you.'

'Oh, have you? Been assessing my character?'

Now she made no answer, but inked in a bar of quavers, testing the phrase on the piano.

'Finish that line of whatever it is and come down to the shore.'

She could hardly believe her ears. He was inviting her to walk with him down to the beach. She wanted to jump up, throw aside the work, dance towards him, fling her arms around his neck and say it was the most delightful suggestion she had heard for a long time.

But she restrained herself, digging the nails of her left hand into her palm. 'And what about your father's compositions?'

'He told me you were working overtime quite needlessly.'

So his father had told him where she was and what she was doing. And he had come to see for himself. Her joy was boundless, but she would not yet allow herself to yield quite so complacently.

'I shan't stay here half the night pleading with you to accompany me,' he said crisply. 'Come now or forget it.'

She put down the pen and rose slowly. 'Perhaps I *could* do with some fresh air.'

She walked with him across the garden and down through the wooded path to the sea. She was treading on air, she felt like a feather, she wanted to skip beside Bryden as a small child might, hopping and dancing for sheer happiness.

Sunset glinted the water to mauve and purple and the rocky point at one end of the little bay was etched sharply against the brilliant light.

Bryden had not spoken much on the way down from the house, except to talk of trivialities, but after a short stroll along the beach, he stopped and pointed to a boulder that made a convenient seat. 'Let's sit down.'

She did so calmly, but inwardly she was all churned up with anticipation. What was he going to tell her?

For a long time he did not tell her anything at all, merely sat in silence, smoking a pipe and gazing at the darkening sea.

'Will you be sorry to leave Corsica in the autumn?'

His question was an anti-climax. She had been expecting —well, she hardly knew exactly what she had been expecting, but certainly not that banal query, on the same level as 'Do you come here often?' Yet perhaps it was more relevant to his thoughts than she imagined.

'Yes, I shall. I enjoy working for your father and Gabrielle. Marguerite has been very kind to me.' She had the impression that her words were almost those of a farewell letter.

'But I've disappointed you.' He made the flat statement without a hint of query in his tone.

Disappointment was not the word she would have used. Anguish and a forlorn hopelessness for the future were the emotions that would be uppermost in her mind on the day of her departure from Corsica.

'No, not particularly. Why should I be disappointed?' She had to make an effort to sound casual and unconcerned. 'I wasn't expecting any—er—special treatment from anyone in the family.'

He turned towards her. Was this the moment when he would take her in his arms and declare his love for her?

'You're a strange girl. Sometimes you seem to me no older than Gabrielle, then you change into a sophisticated woman of the world.'

She stared at him in amazement. 'And which rôle am I playing now?'

'That's it! You're acting all the time. I wonder if anyone ever sees the real Lexa, the girl you really are.'

'But surely no one is ever just one person. We have

138

facets to our personalities and display the one that perhaps subconsciously we think is appropriate to each other person we meet.'

He did not answer and she continued, 'You must admit that you're not the same man to everyone. Your business associates, your father, Marguerite, Gabrielle and——' She was about to add Suzanne, but he forestalled her.

'And you?'

She laughed to hide her uncertainty. 'I don't know what you're like when you're with all those other people.'

'And you of course are different when you're with Philippe? Or that Italian chap, Stefano?'

Oh, really, how blind could you be? she thought angrily. Of course I'm different. They're nonentities—and you, Bryden, are the one man who means anything to me at all.

In a spirit of bravado she answered, 'Perhaps you'd better watch me secretly when I'm with Philippe.'

'I think I'd rather see you with him than with that Italian no-good. Lexa, don't let him impress you with his Latin flattery and ardent looks. I don't know how long you've known him or whether you know much about him, but he's the sort that will break your heart, if you let him. Probably rob you of your handbag if he had the chance.'

'You seem to have formed a very low estimation of his character,' she retorted.

'And have you formed a very high one?' he asked sharply.

She had only to declare now that Stefano was not *her* friend, but Gabrielle's, that she had met him only once for a brief hour and hoped not to see him again unless for the protection of Gabrielle. She did none of these things, for Gabrielle was defenceless and needed Lexa's loyalty until the matter could be straightened out.

'If you invited me to come down here for the purpose of reading me a lecture about my friends or acquaintances, then you could have saved yourself the trouble.' She was angry and spots of colour burned on her cheeks as she faced him. 'I think I can rely on myself to be a judge of men, but maybe I was wrong in my assessment of you.'

'Oh? And how have I fallen short?' She studied the way

his brown hair fell over his forehead, the straight nose, the mobile mouth that could lift in an amused smile or harden into a disapproving line. But it was his grey eyes that now pierced her with grief, for they were icy, almost opaque as though a curtain had fallen over them.

She rose in a jerky, hurried movement and almost tripped over the stones at her feet, but recovered her balance before he could stretch out an arm to save her. That would have been fatal, for he would immediately have jumped to the conclusion that she had stumbled deliberately in order to fall into his arms.

'No sense in talking about it any more,' she threw over her shoulder at him. 'Perhaps I thought you were more like your father.'

She hurried along the beach and towards the path through the woods, aware as always of the scents of the *maquis*, particularly at dusk when the aromatic shrubs and bushes, juniper and rosemary, myrtle and lavender and many others floated their perfumes on the air. The scented island, they called it, but to Lexa it would always be the island where she had known the bitterness of loving a man who had no use for her love.

CHAPTER EIGHT

During the next few days Lexa frequently considered her position in the Frankland household. She was happy enough practising with Gabrielle or copying Edgar's scores; Marguerite was a kind and gracious hostess and all the surroundings were as interesting as anyone could wish.

But Bryden's presence threw a shadow over Lexa's entire peace of mind. While it was true that he was frequently absent for two or three days at a stretch, he was never away long enough for her to try to put him out of her mind. When he was not at home, the house seemed dimmed and when he came back she became nervous and edgy wondering what new fault he would find in her.

When she sat quietly by herself either in her own room or out of doors, she speculated on the question of leaving Corsica and going home as soon as possible. But what reasons could she give Edgar for letting him down? He had engaged her for Gabrielle as accompanist and possibly the break would interfere with Gabrielle's chances of study at the Paris Conservatoire.

As to his own work, there again he depended on her to some extent to assist him in the preparation of his scores for the printers. To go home before the autumn date would be to leave him in the lurch.

It was a welcome diversion when one day Suzanne telephoned to Lexa that the new dress was ready for fitting.

'When will you come?'

The date was fixed and Lexa chose the Friday when Gabrielle would be in Sartène, but there would be no question of Lexa seeing Stefano.

Suzanne called for Lexa in the morning and when the two girls arrived as Suzanne's home, Lexa noticed afresh the dilapidated state of the house.

'Why don't you paint the place up a bit?' she said in a friendly manner. 'I know it's not my business, but the house is going to rack and ruin for want of a lick of paint or a coat of whitewash.'

Suzanne laughed. 'As long as the roof does not leak or the walls blow down, my father thinks it good enough for us.'

'But surely Philippe could do some repairs? Or doesn't he want to soil his hands?'

'Oh, he is always too busy to do simple work like that. As for me, I shall be married and have a house of my own, so there is nothing to worry about.'

Lexa inspected the woodwork of the windows, so flaked and peeled off that it was hard to tell what had been the original colour.

'Buy some paint, Suzanne, and I'll help you to do some decorating. At home I helped my aunt to paint her house.'

Suzanne thought the suggestion a joke. Then she

frowned. 'I don't think my father would give me the money for paint.'

'All right then, I'll ask Edgar if he has any tins knocking around in the garage or outhouses. Perhaps you even have some here yourself. What colour would you like?'

'Scarlet and blue and emerald green,' giggled Suzanne.

'You'll get cream and like it,' threatened Lexa.

They went indoors and upstairs to Suzanne's room, where the tacked-up dress was draped on a fitting model.

'Oh, it looks lovely already!' exclaimed Lexa, viewing the softly draped bodice and the flowing lines of the skirt.

Suzanne took immense trouble with the intricacies of fitting the dress exactly to Lexa's slender figure.

'You have a very slim waist,' observed Suzanne, her mouth full of pins. 'Me, I shall grow plump and like a soft cushion when I am forty.'

Lexa turned obediently for Suzanne to check the hem length. 'There! Now you can take it off and I shall finish it quite soon.'

The dress was full length and would serve as a summer evening dress or could be worn for dinner dates, and Lexa was quite delighted with Suzanne's skill.

'It's very good of you to take so much trouble for me,' she said. 'But you must let me make some return. A gift, perhaps, if not actual money for making?'

'I make dresses for the pleasure.'

Some time later after lunch when the two girls were lazing in very old chairs made of plaited chestnut wood, chairs which Lexa expected to fall apart if carelessly handled, she said, 'Suzanne, why don't you try making beautiful dresses for extra money? You sew so well that surely people would be glad to have them made by you.'

'And where are the people?' queried Suzanne. 'Here, there are few houses between us and Sartène.'

'Oh, I don't mean only private people, but make for the shops—in Sartène, Propriano, Ajaccio, everywhere.'

Suzanne remained silent for a minute or two and Lexa could see that the girl was interested. 'But who would buy the dresses?'

'You'd find it simple to start, I think. Suppose you made up two dresses in your own size as samples and took them to one of the fashion shops in Sartène. Then they could either sell those two dresses, or you would make others to the customers' own measurements. You can't really lose.'

Suzanne's face was still slightly worried and Lexa had an inspiration. 'Look, Suzanne, if you won't let me pay you for my dress, then let me buy you the material for two that you can make up as you choose. Even if nothing came of the idea, you'd still have two pretty dresses.'

'I may think about it,' was all Suzanne would promise. After a pause she asked, 'What sort of outfit will you choose for your wedding?'

The question took Lexa by surprise as she had not been contemplating wedding dresses lately, viewing such clothes as only a most remote possibility.

'Wedding? Oh, I don't know.'

'But when you go home to England, you will prepare to marry Clifford, is it not?'

Lexa shook her head. 'No. It was all settled before he went home——'

'Then you have fixed the date?'

'No, no, Suzanne, you don't understand. Clifford and I were not engaged and we broke off any—well, slight understanding we might have had.'

The change in Suzanne's demeanour was dramatic. She shot up from her chair and the sudden movement caused part of the armpiece to break and hang lopsidedly. 'But you told me! You declared that you were here for only a few months, then you would go home and marry him.'

'I said nothing of the kind. You assumed it was so.'

'So you changed your mind. Also, you stayed at the inn in the mountains with Bryden, so that you thought he would have to marry you.'

'Oh, for goodness' sake! I told you that there was no compulsion for that to happen at all.'

'Oh, it is very disagreeable that I like you, Lexa, for I must learn to hate you all the time!' burst out Suzanne. 'I will never let you have Bryden. He loves me and I must have him.'

'Poor Bryden!' murmured Lexa, not taking this outburst too seriously. Suzanne's tantrums did not usually last long.

'Oh, yes, "poor Bryden"—that is indeed so when an English girl comes here and steals him from me. But you will see! I shall win in the end, and you'll have to go home to England and then perhaps you might be glad to marry your Clifford.'

'A week or two ago you were keen for me to marry your brother,' pointed out Lexa when Suzanne had paused for breath.

'No. That would not be suitable now—for I would not like to have you here on the island at all. I like you better far away.'

'Then wait patiently for the autumn and I shall be gone,' returned Lexa, reflecting that when she left Corsica she would leave behind a precious dream, a rosy haze of what-might-have-been.

But now Blanche, the housekeeper, came out with a tray of hot chocolate and a plate of tiny cakes that were crisp and golden and decorated with nuts. Suzanne resumed her chair and angrily pulled off the broken arm.

When an hour or so later Lexa suggested leaving, Suzanne agreed without fuss this time to drive to Fontenay, but Lexa was none too confident in the driver's competence. Suzanne drove very fast at all times, regardless of hairpin bends or steep tracks, Philippe's car was a ramshackle old vehicle and tonight, in addition, Suzanne was in a mood of smouldering resentment.

It was certainly no relief to Lexa when Suzanne said crossly, 'If I were not a kind person, I could make an accident and push you over the edge of the mountain. But I have no sense for what is best for me.'

Lexa glanced at her companion. 'If you ran the car over the edge, what would happen to you? Or would you jump out and save yourself?'

Suzanne shrugged and took the next bend at increased speed, but Lexa refused to show fear or nervousness. Yet

144

one small incident demonstrated that the French girl's threats might have at least some substance.

Lexa had alighted in the courtyard of Fontenay and after finishing her conversation with Suzanne about the dress and when it would be finished, she suggested, 'Are you coming in to see Madame Frankland?'

Suzanne hesitated. 'Is Bryden at home?'

'I don't know. He was away all this week—and I don't see his car.'

'Then I will go home,' decided Suzanne. Lexa was reaching into the car where she had left her jacket on the back seat. As she straightened, the door on Suzanne's side swung shut with a violent bang. Only seconds before, Lexa's fingers had been holding on to the side of the car. If she had not released them, they might have been crushed.

She stared at Suzanne. 'You nearly jammed my fingers in your door,' said Lexa, not caring whether her words sounded accusing.

Suzanne continued to smile blandly. 'But they are not hurt,' she answered placidly, as she drove off.

Lexa, watching the car turn, wondered if Suzanne had added in her mind, 'Not this time.'

An injured left hand would certainly cripple her chances of remaining to work with Gabrielle. Lexa sighed, as she went into the house. She was becoming suspicious, distrusting other people and their motives for inadequate reasons.

When Gabrielle returned from Sartène, she came into the music practice room where Lexa was at the piano.

'So now you have made a new conquest,' she said, with a puckish grin.

'Oh? Who this time?'

'Don't pretend! Stefano, of course. When I saw him today, he was no longer interested in me. He wanted to know where the so charming English girl was.'

'I went to Suzanne's house.'

'I am quite pushed aside in favour of you,' grumbled Gabrielle, but Lexa imagined that she heard in the other girl's tone a certain resignation without rancour. Had Gabrielle perhaps seen for herself that Stefano was unreliable and easily attracted to other girls and that his protestations of devotion were worthless? Lexa sincerely hoped so.

At dinner that evening Bryden came in when the meal was almost finished.

'We have missed you!' greeted Gabrielle sarcastically.

As he passed her chair he rumpled her hair. Lexa was immediately filled with envy, wishing that Bryden's hand would fondle her head like that, but she pushed aside the stupid thoughts and listened to the conversation that was going on between Bryden and his father, with Marguerite putting in an occasional question.

It seemed that Bryden had satisfactorily concluded the business transaction of purchasing the neglected little inn at Calveroso in the mountains. Lexa's face reddened at the memory of that place where she had been forced to spend a night along with Bryden when the road home was blocked. She wondered now while he was talking whether the inn had any significance for him or whether he regarded it, apart from the purchase, as a spot where Lexa had behaved in a stupid and shameful manner.

'The one small fly in the ointment,' he was saying now, 'is that I can't find out who owns a piece of land between the inn and the other piece of ground at the back. Unless we can get both pieces, one isn't much good without the other. We can't have a gap in between and then a year or two ahead someone comes along and puts up a building we don't like.'

'No, I can see the difficulty,' agreed Edgar. 'Is there no record of the owners?'

'I've asked the lawyers to look into the matter, but usually you can find out these things in the village itself. Someone always knows whose grandfather bought the plot, who sold it and to whom, but in Calveroso everyone has sewn up his lips—unless there's a conspiracy of silence.'

'Perhaps there's something wrong with the land?' suggested Marguerite.

'Or a legend about it,' put in Gabrielle. 'Like a murder— or a vendetta started there.'

'Or there's a ghostly violin-player on the Eve of St John,' Bryden threw back at her. He turned towards Lexa. 'Come, Lexa, haven't you a conjecture to add to the rest? Have a go.'

Her face flamed at his invitation, for she guessed that he was baiting her yet again. 'I don't think I saw the plot of land you mean, unless it was what looked like a small field.' Then she added with a touch of spirit, 'Perhaps it belongs to someone who is determined to make you pay a high price for it, if he knows it's really necessary for you to have it.'

Bryden rewarded her with a broad grin, but his eyes held a mocking light. 'Well said, Lexa! The only sensible explanation! It's more than likely that half the men in the village have been promised a rake-off from the profit, if they keep their mouths shut.'

No more was said about the plot of land and the talk turned towards the forthcoming recital that was to take place in Ajaccio, when Marguerite would play cello sonatas, Gabrielle would join in trios with Lexa and Edgar would give piano solos of two new compositions.

Marguerite and Gabrielle had performed on several occasions in Ajaccio and other parts of the island, as well as in Paris, but to Lexa this was an entirely new experience and she looked forward to it with combined enthusiasm and trepidation. Much depended on her as accompanist and she hoped that she would not fail her fellow-musicians.

For the next few days she and Gabrielle practised assiduously, with Lexa correcting the younger girl's faults of pitch or tempo. Then there were sessions with Marguerite for cello practice, when Lexa needed all her concentration, for Marguerite was not only a professional, but a perfectionist and every nuance, every phrasing had to be polished to the highest degree.

Edgar arranged for a dress rehearsal two nights before the recital, but to Lexa's discomfiture, not only was Bryden present, but Suzanne and Philippe came. The object of Suzanne's visit had ostensibly been to bring the dress she had made for Lexa, but she and her brother eagerly stayed to dinner.

'It will be a gala night for us,' declared Philippe, although of course he would also be in the audience at the actual concert.

When Lexa sat at the piano to open with a Chopin prelude, Philippe drew up a chair on her left. 'I'll turn the pages for you,' he offered.

'No score for this,' she answered, glad to reject his offer. 'I've learnt it to play from memory.'

'Oh!' His face fell with disappointment. Then he said brightly, 'But I can still sit here to give you encouragement.'

She turned towards him, acutely aware that Bryden was watching her. 'Look, Philippe, I'm sorry, but I can't bear anyone to sit next to me at the piano. Please sit a little distance away—where I can't see you.'

'Brother, how you are set down!' said Bryden mockingly, with a glance at Lexa that she was unsure how to interpret. Was it approval that she had slightly snubbed Philippe or satisfaction that he himself had not been the victim of her acid tongue?

With Gabrielle and Marguerite, she progressed through the programme and Edgar reserved his comments until the end. Encouragement for Gabrielle, mixed with a word or two of criticism. For Lexa nothing but praise, most of which she thought she did not deserve.

Even Bryden sounded complimentary, although Lexa could never be sure how sincere he might be. Much later, after Philippe and Suzanne had returned home and the rest of the family were sitting outside on the terrace for a breath of fresh air before bedtime, Lexa was collecting the sheet music and sorting it into the instrumental parts. Bryden leaned over the farther edge of the grand piano.

'You really enjoy giving your time to music, don't you?'

She looked up quickly, then down again, for his scrutiny disturbed her so much that she felt weak and helpless. 'Naturally I enjoy it. Otherwise I wouldn't be here.'

'I've changed my opinion about you,' he went on. 'I don't think you're the opportunist I took you for when you first came.'

'Could I ask what has brought about this dramatic change?'

'What a vinegary girl you are! First you slap down Philippe—although I can't exactly lament about him. Now I have only to say a kind word and you fly at my throat.'

'And what am I expected to do when you fling me a kind word? Smile shyly and curtsey?'

Bryden gave a short, explosive laugh. 'Such a picture of you is beyond imagination. You're too prickly. Or,' he added as an afterthought, 'perhaps you're not so prickly towards other people.'

Lexa drew in her breath sharply. Of course he was right. Couldn't the blind fool see that it was her deep and overwhelming love for him that made her lash out with unamiable remarks?

'Perhaps other people don't bait me as much as you do,' she returned steadily.

'Bait you?' he echoed. 'Tell me when I have ever done that?'

'All the time! Either I'm an opportunist sheltering in your father's house, accepting his generosity, or I'm a heartless flirt eager for all the attention I can get from men!'

'But I've just told you that I'd changed my opinion——'

'Oh, I know what you *said*. It's what you *think* that matters.'

He came towards her. 'Does it matter to you, Lexa, what I think?'

There was a softness in his tone that she had never heard before. She was so close to him that if she turned she would be in his arms, but she was not to be caught that way again. Always before her inner vision was that scene in the bedroom of the inn at Calveroso, where she had melted into his embrace with such shameful responsiveness towards a man who cared nothing at all for her.

So now she took a step backwards and faced him with a forced anger that she did not really feel, for all her senses cried out to her to yield. 'All that matters to me is that I fulfil the task I came to do, and do it well. After that,

149

it won't bother me what you think.'

She bent to put away the music into the cabinet and when she straightened up, she saw his hand stretch out towards her. His touch on her wrist sent the fire burning again in her whole body, but now she exerted all her self-control and snatched her wrist away.

'I'll try to keep the peace while I live in your father's house,' she said, tears almost choking her voice, 'but don't make it so difficult for me.'

Without looking at him again she ran from the room and tore upstairs to her bedroom. Why did he tempt her so much? All he wanted, it seemed, was to encourage her to make a fool of herself, not once, but over and over again, and she vowed that she would not give him that satisfaction.

A few minutes later she went out on to her balcony. Below she could hear voices, Edgar's and Bryden's. The two men were strolling in the garden under her windows. She could not distinguish what they were saying, but she thought she caught the word 'Lexa'. It was too dark to see their figures, but Bryden's presence floated up to her. Yet again she asked herself why she had been so foolish as to fall so hopelessly in love with him when there was obviously no possibility of her love being returned.

She knew that he was not wholly indifferent to her, but after his tragic experiences with two other girls in his life, perhaps now he was seeking only easy conquests with no permanent ties.

For Lexa there was no easy satisfaction, for a brief affair would have meant even more heartache than the realisation that in due course the irrevocable parting would come and her own future and that of Bryden would travel along widely separated paths.

CHAPTER NINE

EDGAR arranged for his family with Lexa to stay at one of the Ajaccio hotels on the day of the recital.

'You can relax there, lounge about, swim in the pool and be fresh for the evening, without any last-minute practices,' he told Gabrielle and Lexa. 'We'll come home next day at our leisure.'

Edgar drove the two girls and Bryden was to come later with Marguerite and her cello. Lexa was both disappointed and glad simultaneously, but on balance she decided that it was best not to see Bryden too often and certainly not be alone with him.

Lexa would have been glad of a rehearsal in the hall where the recital was to take place, but Edgar assured her that the acoustics were very good.

'It isn't the same as playing with an orchestra. Then you really need to get the feel of the hall and where the sound is coming from.'

During the afternoon Lexa and Gabrielle relaxed in the spacious grounds of the hotel, where there were delightful gardens and a swimming pool, although the sea was only a few yards away with an attractive beach.

At dinner served specially early in a private room, Gabrielle declared that she was much too nervous to eat.

'Nonsense!' scolded her mother gently. 'You are not singing, merely holding a violin, and we shall not expect you to fall down in the middle of a sonata fainting from hunger.'

'You've given recitals in public already,' said Lexa slightly reproachfully, 'but for me this is my first real appearance. Nothing more than small local concerts before or playing at a club dinner. So you have more experience than I.'

'Don't worry,' counselled Marguerite. 'You'll be all right as soon as you sit down at the piano and strike the first notes.'

That advice proved to be correct, for Lexa's nervousness

vanished with the first bars of her opening prelude. Her new dress, made by Suzanne, also gave her confidence, for she knew that her appearance was not disgracing her two fellow-musicians, Gabrielle in white chiffon embroidered with small golden beads, and her mother in a sumptuous gown of deep sapphire brocade, the skirts flowing around her as she sat with her cello.

The programme devised by Edgar, ranging through Brahms and Haydn trios, sonatas by Debussy and Mozart, seemed to be well received, particularly Edgar's own new compositions. Lexa was given the honour of the final items and played Spanish dances by Granados. As she stood on the platform to receive the applause, she was conscious of a thrill of achievement. At least she had not let down her companions.

In the artistes' room, Edgar patted her on the back and smiled at her with genuine approval. 'You did marvellously well, Lexa. Beautiful performances in your solos and nicely controlled in the trios and sonatas. We must drink to your further success.'

He grabbed a glass of champagne from a passing waiter and handed it to her. 'To your future success as a pianist! You must launch out on your own in due course.'

She laughed, then sipped the champagne and as she half turned, she caught sight of herself in a large gilded mirror. For once, she thought, I don't look too bad, even if that's sheer vanity. Suzanne had made a wonderful job of the dress and the simple flowing style accentuated the beautiful fabric and design of bronze leaves and cream background; the pale green splashes of colour echoed her grey-green eyes and the wisps of flame toned with her bronze hair, brushed tonight into shoulder-length curves.

Then suddenly over her shoulder she saw Bryden's reflection in the mirror. She had not even known if he was in the audience, for several times during the performance she had raked the rows of concertgoers in vain for a glimpse of him.

Now she turned almost in panic and so sharply that splashes of champagne fell on her dress.

'There! Careless girl!' he greeted her. 'Look what you've done—and such a pretty dress. Still, champagne never stains. No lasting effects—like a holiday romance.'

At his first words her spirits had lifted, for he appeared to be in a lighthearted mood, but that final phrase—'no lasting effects—like a holiday romance' fell like ice on her consciousness.

She schooled herself to ask, 'Did you think the recital went well?' Then she smiled and added, 'Or weren't you in the hall? I suppose the programme wasn't really to your taste.'

'On the contrary,' he said quickly, 'I was there from your opening passage, gazing from afar and wondering how you could remember which note to play when you hadn't the score in front of you.'

'Oh, even with Chopin, one finds a sort of catchy tune that one can remember,' she replied airily.

'I really think, Lexa, that one day you'll have to take me in hand and educate me musically, so that I know a crotchet from a crowbar.'

She laughed. 'Or a semiquaver from a shiver?' Perhaps it was the headiness of her own good performance as well as the champagne that enabled her to continue this delicious fooling, for she would not let herself think of a prospect where she would hold Bryden's hand either physically or metaphorically and instruct him in the mysteries of music appreciation.

He had seized another bottle of champagne and filled her glass anew. He stood looking down at her with an expression in his eyes that filled her with delight, for it was both tender and challenging at the same time, mischievous, yet good-natured and without malice.

Then he lifted his own glass. 'To your success, Lexa,' he said softly, 'and complete happiness.'

She was touched by his apparent sincerity and with slightly trembling lips murmured 'Thank you' and sipped her champagne.

When she looked around the room she saw that most of the people had drifted away. 'Come, Lexa,' Bryden murmured, 'we must go—or they will lock us in for the night.'

Such a prospect with Bryden as her companion seemed to her the epitome of delight, but she steadied herself to dismiss these wild fancies. Yet as he piloted her out of the room, along a passage and down some steps to the street, his arm was around her shoulders, his hand warm on the top of her arm. She walked with him in step, neither leaning too obviously against him or drawing herself away. This must be a dream, surely! It wasn't really happening. She was in bed at Fontenay, weaving this fantastic illusion. Then she glanced down at her new dress, touched the folds, and revelled in the reality of the moment.

Then a harsher reality broke in, for Philippe and Suzanne were outside and somehow she was separated from Bryden, practically pushed into a car and driven back to the hotel where the Frankland party were staying overnight.

Edgar had arranged a reception in a private room for some of his friends who had attended the concert and Lexa found herself pitchforked into a whole company of people enjoying a buffet meal. Marguerite and Gabrielle were surrounded by a knot of enthusiastic admirers, Edgar was talking to several men. Bryden seemed to have disappeared. Suddenly in the midst of this gathering, the realisation swept over Lexa that she was very much the outsider. The others belonged to their own small circles and to the island while she was no more than a temporary visitor.

Philippe came across the room towards her. 'Lexa! You are all alone! But this must not happen.'

He flung an arm around her waist and guided her towards the buffet tables, but then just as Lexa helped herself to a couple of canapés, Suzanne came rushing up excitedly. 'Come on! We're all going swimming—in the moonlight.'

There was a general exodus of most of the younger people, but Lexa hesitated. Philippe took her arm. 'You would like to swim by night—or shall we perhaps find a comfortable corner in the gardens? The moon will shine just as well on us as on the others in the water.'

Lexa was faced with a difficult choice. This was almost literally between the devil and the deep blue sea, if Philippe could be termed 'the devil', and she had no desire for a romantic interlude with him. If Bryden had offered such a choice——? But that would never have happened, of course.

'I'll swim, I think,' she decided. 'I feel rather sleepy, so it will liven me up.'

Lexa had been unsure whether the bathing party would be in the hotel pool or the sea, but the pool was silent, so she walked the short distance down to the shore. Suzanne came hurrying behind her. 'This is a delightful experience for you?' she asked.

'Well, yes. I've never swum in the dark before.'

'It is very amusing. Sometimes you can be embraced in the water—and never know who——'

'I thought you were quite shocked by such behaviour,' Lexa teased, remembering Suzanne's criticism of English girls.

Suzanne pushed back her flowing golden hair and smiled mischievously. 'It depends—who——'

There were perhaps a dozen people in the water, laughing and splashing about. Lexa dropped her wrap on to the beach and plunged into the dark gentle waves. It was indeed, as Suzanne had said, a delightful experience to glide about on the silver-glinting surface, then turn away to shadowed depths.

Half a dozen swimmers were indulging in a game that involved joining hands in the middle of a ring, then trying to revolve clockwise. 'Come, Lexa!' invited Suzanne, making a place for her. Philippe was next to his sister and then Lexa saw Bryden on the far side of the ring. Someone shouted, *'Tournez! Un! Deux! Trois!'* and the group began to revolve slowly, then quickened speed until the circle broke apart in a tangle of arms and legs. Lexa was pushed underwater by someone's flailing arm, then when she tried to rise, found herself pinned down. She struggled frantically to jerk herself up, but the unseen assailant did not release her. She flung up her arms and kicked out with her feet, twisting, trying to turn, striving to get her head out of the water. Suddenly the relentless hold on the back of her neck was relaxed and she came to the surface, choking and spluttering.

Lexa saw then that the moon had disappeared behind a cloud and the sun-warmed water was dark, too dark to distinguish the other swimmers or where they were. After a moment or two while she recovered her breath she saw some of the party walking up the beach and with speedy strokes she swam to the edge of the shore.

Someone evidently had some peculiar ideas of what could be termed gentle horse-play. Lexa did not pretend to be an expert swimmer, and to be held under water for what seemed an eternity was not exactly a joke. The beach was still warm with the heat of the day, but she shivered as she towelled herself, then donned her wrap. Whose was the hand that had held her so menacingly?

A few people were still in the water, for she could hear their shouts and laughter, but there was no sign of Philippe or Suzanne—or Bryden.

She hurried towards the hotel gardens, too shaken by this unnerving experience to wait for anyone to accompany her. Was it merely someone with a crooked sense of humour who guessed it would be fun to hold down a girl with her head under water? Or was it someone who really wanted her out of the way, someone clever enough to make the incident look like an unlucky accident.

She stopped dead on the path, a wave of horror engulfing her. Bryden's second tragic loss! His fiancée had been drowned in a swimming pool. But where was the possible connection? Where was the motive? She leaned against the trunk of a palm tree. No one had a motive for trying to do away with her—except Suzanne? But Suzanne would have had to exert great strength to hold another girl down in the buoyant Mediterranean.

Slowly she resumed walking towards the hotel entrance, then a tall shadow emerged from the bushes. She gave a muffled exclamation of fright and was almost ready to run when Bryden spoke.

'Lexa!'

The way he murmured her name shattered the tautness

of her self-control and she burst into tears.

'What is it? What's the matter?' His hands were on her shoulders, he was drawing her close to him, and her bones turned to water.

'I—I was afraid,' she sobbed brokenly. 'Someone—was —trying to—to drown me——'

The moon emerged from the clouds and as she glanced up she saw his face dramatised in the silver light, the angles of his cheekbone and jaw, the deep shadows where his eyes were veiled, the untidy mop of brown hair, still wet from swimming.

'What on earth——' Then he held her close to him, his chin on her hair, her body against his naked chest as his towelling wrap fell open. 'Who would want to drown you?' He lifted her chin and his lips pressed on hers, forestalling any reply she might have made. She gave herself up to the idyllic moment, aware only that she was in the haven of Bryden's arms and nothing else mattered as he muttered soothing words, kissing her for punctuation, rocking her to and fro as one might comfort a stricken child.

'Lexa, don't tempt me,' he whispered. 'I'm only flesh and blood.'

For answer, she pressed herself against him, her arms entwined around his neck.

Shouts and mocking laughter recalled them to present reality and as Lexa sharply turned, she saw a group of people coming along the path, Suzanne and Philippe among them.

Appalled at being surprised in such circumstances and aware of her scanty attire, only bikini and bathing wrap, she disengaged herself from Bryden and fled precipitately towards the hotel, would not wait for the lift, but raced up the stairs to her room.

It had been a night of enchantment and fright, rapture and suspicion, and finally delight which not even the humiliation of discovery could quench.

Lexa showered and was already in bed when a tap at the door alerted her. A moment later Suzanne entered.

Lexa warily waited for the other to speak. 'Swimming

157

has tired you?' Suzanne asked, flinging herself into the armchair near the bed.

'I've had a long day,' replied Lexa. 'The recital was very important to me—to all of us.'

'Naturally. When you go back to England, you will be famous, eh?'

Lexa smiled. 'I should hardly think so.' She changed the subject abruptly. 'How have you got on with the sample dresses you were designing for the shops?'

Lexa had already supplied two lengths of material to Suzanne's choice and the girl had bought several others.

Suzanne shrugged. 'It is only a game,' she answered. 'Why should I spend my time trying to make money when soon it will all come to me with no trouble?'

'Why? Are you expecting to come into a fortune?'

'My fortune will come, you will see,' Suzanne said with a spurt of impatience.

Lexa made a great pretence of yawning, impolite though it might be. 'Forgive me, Suzanne, but I'm very sleepy.' Then a thought occurred to her. 'Are you staying in the hotel overnight?'

'No. Philippe will drive us home, but he is now in the bar with several other men he knows.' After a moment she added, 'The swimming games, you enjoyed them?'

Lexa sat up straighter among the pillows. 'I did *not* enjoy being pushed under the water. Someone held me under for what seemed a long time.'

Suzanne's dark eyes rounded in surprise. 'You are making a joke?'

'Indeed, not. Perhaps it was accidental, but I don't think so.'

Suzanne smiled thoughtfully. 'Who would want you to be drowned? Perhaps you are not a good swimmer?'

'Not really very expert, but—oh, never mind.' Lexa did not want to pursue the subject, but Suzanne had other ideas.

'You know, perhaps, that—Bryden—his girl-friend was drowned, no one knew how. Was he near you when you were pushed down?'

'I've no idea,' snapped Lexa.

Suzanne rose. 'Poor Bryden! So unlucky with women. But soon more lucky. I must go now, for Philippe won't know where I am. Goodnight, Lexa.'

'Goodnight, Suzanne.'

Suzanne turned as she reached the door. 'Perhaps poor Bryden does not know how to get rid of girls he does not love. If someone is drowned, then it is accident—naturally.'

The door closed before Lexa could reply, but what could she have said? Sleep evaded her for a long time and when she finally dozed off, her dreams were haunted by someone pushing her down into a dark abyss, Suzanne's smiling face taunting her through a haze of water, Bryden pushing her away from him so that she fell into yet another kind of black nothingness.

Next morning she was glad to relax in the car along with Gabrielle while Edgar drove back to Fontenay. Lexa had come to love the craggy landscape of the island, the silvery olives, the pine trees, most of all the perfume of the maquis drifting through the window. The scented island was one place she would never forget.

For the next couple of days there was mild excitement in the household waiting for the newspaper notices of the recital. Marguerite searched assiduously through *Nice-Matin* and cut out the half column which praised without stint Edgar's own new compositions and touched briefly on the other items.

'"Madame Frankland played with a mature sureness of touch," ' she quoted, laughing. 'Soon I shall be so old that my bow will quiver of its own accord on the strings!'

Gabrielle received what Edgar called 'adequate' press notices, but Lexa was awarded compliments for her sympathetic accompaniments.

'Now,' Edgar instructed, 'you must tackle new works.' He mapped out a programme for practice, including a Bartok Rhapsody and works by Bach, Stravinsky, Mendelssohn and Britten. 'Those should give you both plenty of variety.'

Lexa was glad of the chance to throw herself into music

practice, for Bryden was away from home and she had not seen him since the night of the recital. She wondered what his attitude would be when next she saw him, and by now her elation over that brief garden encounter when he had held her so lovingly in his arms had evaporated in the uncertainty of never being able to guess his next reaction.

On the other hand, Philippe called every day on some pretext or other.

'That's a very good idea of yours, Lexa,' he said one afternoon. 'About painting up our place, I mean. It could certainly do with some renovation.'

'You could probably spare the time,' she answered with a sardonic glance and a smile. 'You don't seem to work too hard at whatever it is you do. Your spare time seems unlimited.'

Philippe shrugged his slim shoulders. 'Not everyone can dig the ground or spray the vines. There are other ways of earning money. I have many friends—and we work together on commission.'

She did not press him for further details, since his way of living was not at all her concern.

The following weekend he asked if she would be ready to help with the painting. 'Suzanne says you offered in the first place.'

She hesitated. 'I offered to help her, certainly, but surely you can do the job by yourself.' She was not anxious to spend time at the Morianis' house.

Philippe gave her one of his most winning smiles. 'Come this first time anyway, for you can help me with the paints, the colour scheme. Also, Suzanne has some dresses to show you and she would like to have your advice.'

On arrival at the house, she soon discovered that Suzanne was absent.

'Ah, yes,' Philippe replied when she asked him about his sister, 'she went up to one of the mountain villages with my father.'

But although Philippe implied that Suzanne had left only that day, Blanche, the housekeeper, told Lexa that the girl had gone two days ago.

160

So Philippe had lied about Suzanne wanting to show the dresses, and did not even trouble to deny the fact when she accused him.

'What does it matter?' he asked, putting a companionable arm around her shoulders and kissing the tip of her ear. 'If you worry about being alone here with me, then there is nothing to be afraid of. Blanche is here all the time.'

But Lexa was still dubious and wished fervently that she had never consented to come.

'Let's get on with the painting, then,' she said briskly. 'That's what I came for.'

'I hope not only the painting,' he said meaningly.

He had found several half-empty pots of paint in an outhouse and had bought one new tin of white.

'These pots need to be stirred, the paint is all lumps,' she told him. 'Have you also some brushes?'

He produced an old glass jar containing several brushes stiff and dry with old paint.

'No use,' she said. 'These must have been used to paint Noah's Ark—and never cleaned since.'

'But, darling Lexa, there are no others,' he complained.

'You should have bought at least one new brush with the paint.'

'The man who gave me the paint didn't have any spare brushes.'

'Gave you the paint? So you didn't buy it?'

Philippe grinned. 'Who would buy when you can get something another way. It was in return for a service I did for him.'

Lexa knew better than to ask the nature of the service. She had learned that some of his business activities verged on the shady.

'Then we'll have to do the best we can to prepare the surfaces we're going to paint,' she suggested. 'At least we can scrape off the old paint.'

'As you say,' he agreed. 'You're the boss.'

But some of the woodwork, particularly around the windows, was so fragile that the timber fell to pieces at the merest touch.

'You need new window frames,' she told him. 'It's hopeless trying to put paint on that old wood.'

Philippe threw up his hands in despair. 'My father will never spend money on this old place.'

'But you all have to live in it!'

'Not for ever,' he said decisively. 'Suzanne will marry, my father will eventually die—or perhaps in his old age he will go to live in the mountains with others of his family.'

'And you?'

'Ah!' He seized both her hands. 'I shall have a wonderful flat in Ajaccio, superb furniture, every luxury. A place where I can bring my wife. Naturally, I could never bring her to this old wreck.'

'Who will pay for the lovely flat? Or are you looking for a rich wife?'

His dark, handsome face clouded. 'That, of course, is a difficulty. I am hopelessly in love with you, Lexa, but at first we would have to endure something not luxurious.'

She laughed, 'But you don't have to provide for me.'

'But I do, Lexa. I want you so much. I love you more than anyone I've ever met.'

A practised speech, Lexa judged. Such glib phrases came easily to Philippe's tongue. 'Are you asking me to marry you?' she queried, sharply enough to take him by surprise apparently.

'I would not want you to go on working for the Franklands,' he answered, but not yet replying to her question. 'Perhaps you would be able to do something else—find a job—just for a short time, you understand?'

She pulled her hands away from his. 'I see,' she said slowly. 'You're in love enough to ask me to set up house with you—live with you, but marriage doesn't come into it.'

'Oh, I'd marry you—as soon as I could,' he protested.

She shook her head. 'No, Philippe, it wouldn't do for me. I like you, but I don't love you.'

Anger swept over his features. 'You think you're in love with Bryden! You'd marry him if he asked you, wouldn't you? But he won't ask. He has other plans.'

'Let's forget it and start the job,' she said irritably. She was disturbed, as Philippe had known she would be, by that phrase—'he has other plans'. What plans? Another girl? Someone here in Corsica? Or in England? So there was as little substance in Bryden's displays of affection as in Philippe's. At least Philippe was candid about his inability or unwillingness to marry the girl of the moment.

The next hour or so was spent in trying to clean down some of the existing paintwork, the front door, and the outside walls of the house, but Lexa knew she was wasting her time. Nothing short of new windows and doors and re-paired guttering would avail.

At six o'clock she asked Philippe to drive her home to Fontenay.

'Not yet,' he decided.

'I'm expected back to dinner.'

'Blanche is cooking dinner for you here.'

Lexa saw that she had unwittingly walked into a trap. Philippe had no intention of driving her back tonight. She fought down the panic that rose like a tide within her. At all costs, she must keep calm and think of a way out of this unpalatable situation. She was familiar now with the road home, even though it was probably some five or six miles, but if she left now, there would be enough daylight.

'Please give your housekeeper my apologies, but I can't stay,' she said coldly. 'If you won't drive me, I shall walk.'

'Lexa, you can't!' he shouted, as she turned her back on him and began to walk down the untidy, rough path to the road.

Then she heard Blanche's voice speaking in French. 'Let her go! She is English! She will make trouble.'

Lexa looked back over her shoulder, partly to see if Philippe were following, but the woman had laid a restrain-ing hand on his sleeve. Her face held a bitter expression and Lexa knew that Blanche had no affection for her. In this event, Lexa was only too glad of Blanche's loyalty to the Moriani family. Clearly, she did not want Philippe to be mixed up in any trouble with foreign girls.

Lexa stepped out along the road, slightly apprehensive

that at some point Philippe would come behind her, either on foot or in the car, but although a couple of cars passed her going towards Sartène, none followed her.

After a couple of miles she slowed down to watch the sunset over the peaks on her right, the grey rock turning pink and orange, with violet blue chasms between. The *maquis* was fragmented by golden light into separate gleaming bushes standing out among the dark shade.

She walked on and now the road led slightly downhill with a view of the sea. When she heard a car behind her, she pressed herself against the steep, solid rock until it would pass, but it slowed down and voices cried out.

'Lexa! Lexa!'

Bryden was driving and Gabrielle and Marguerite sat in the back. Bryden lowered his window. 'You'll have to come round the other side.' He opened the offside door and she cautiously walked round the front of the car and stepped in. The road was narrow at that point and Bryden had been driving as far away from the precipitous edge as possible.

'Taking an evening walk?' queried Bryden when he started the car again.

'But I thought you went to Suzanne's,' put in Marguerite.

'Yes, I did.'

'Why are you walking home, then?' asked Gabrielle excitedly.

'Philippe's car was troublesome,' Lexa lied smoothly.

'Not surprising,' snapped Bryden. 'If he looked after it better, he wouldn't have so much trouble.'

'But to let you walk—alone—by yourself!' Gabrielle sounded shocked and distressed. 'It is not gallant. He should have accompanied you.'

Lexa smiled, not wanting to say that she had been relieved to lack his company. 'I left him tinkering with the car. He said he might be able to pick me up halfway along this road.'

'But better that we should find you,' interposed Marguerite.

On arrival at Fontenay, Lexa alighted with the others, but Bryden's face was stony. When she thanked him for giving her a lift, he muttered curtly, 'Don't make a habit of walking along that road. It's not suitable for pedestrians.' He slammed the car door and backed the car into the garage.

Could this be the same man who had held her in his arms only a few nights ago, whispered tender, soothing words and kissed away her tears?

He did not put in an appearance at dinner and evidently had a meal served in his study. Next morning he had left the house before Lexa was up.

But for that chance meeting along the road, she would not have seen him. Maybe it would have been better for her if she had arrived home without his help, for then she could have remained a little longer in her fool's paradise. Now her emotions were churned up into a tension that came between her and the occupation of the moment. Gabrielle noticed it at music practice.

'Lexa, you tell me when the notes are wrong. Now *you* are playing wrong ones. That is G sharp.' She pointed with her bow to the stave.

'Sorry. Yes, you're right.'

Two days later Philippe called at Fontenay. He was bubbling with excitement and strode about the terrace, calling 'Lexa! Lexa! Gabrielle! Who is at home?'

Lexa and Gabrielle were practising. 'What is the matter with him?' Gabrielle said irritably. 'Is the house on fire?'

She went down and Lexa followed several minutes later. Marguerite stood by the white-painted iron table on the terrace, her face pale. 'I can't believe it,' she was saying in a low tone. Lexa looked at Gabrielle's incredulous face, then back to Marguerite, then to Philippe, who face showed only the delight and gladness of someone who has received his heart's desire.

'What is it?' queried Lexa. At first, she thought some awful accident had happened to one of the family, but then Philippe would not be looking so immensely pleased.

Gabrielle had turned away, but Philippe grasped Lexa's hands and was almost dancing for joy. 'Bryden is going to marry Suzanne! It is all arranged.'

But for the fact that Philippe was holding her, Lexa would

have swayed and collapsed in a heap on the ground.

'To marry? Suzanne?' she whispered through stiff lips.

'Yes. Oh, my sister is in raptures.'

'Then we are not!' Gabrielle's voice cut angrily across the terrace.

'Gabrielle!' her mother admonished. 'That was rude to Philippe.'

But Gabrielle was defiant. 'I am sorry!' she snapped, going closer to Philippe, 'but not for what I said. Only for Bryden!'

She ran indoors quickly, leaving the others in a frozen tableau, Marguerite now sitting at the table, her dark head bowed, Lexa who had released herself from Philippe, and the young man surveying the two women with an amused expression.

'Would you leave us, please, Philippe?' Marguerite said, some of her normal composure regained.

'But certainly.' He walked jauntily from the terrace towards his car.

'Come with me, Lexa,' Marguerite said to the girl, and led the way into the little private sitting-room that was her own and where none of the rest of the family intruded without invitation.

'This is a great blow to me,' she said.

Lexa said nothing. Her body felt like ice, her eyes were dry, for the tears would fall later.

Marguerite stretched out her hand. 'I can't believe he would be so foolish. I'm sure he doesn't love her.'

Lexa sat beside the older woman on the satin-covered settee.

'It's not like him—to do this.' Marguerite turned towards Lexa. 'Philippe told us that Bryden and Suzanne had stayed together—not one night, but several—at an inn in the mountains, so of course he will marry her.'

'You mean—the Corsican law?'

'Oh, I don't know. That absurd law is out of date now.'

Lexa's numb brain was vaguely remembering Suzanne's conversation after the episode at Calveroso. *You stayed the night at an inn in the mountains. So of course he must marry you. He has no choice*. That was what Suzanne had said, and then later, when Lexa had declared that she and Bryden had not slept in the same room, Suzanne laughed, asking who would believe *that*?

'I had such hopes for Bryden,' Marguerite murmured. 'I love him as my own son and he has had so much unhappiness. I wanted him to find a true, lasting love.'

'But if he really does love Suzanne?' Lexa forced herself to say.

'I know he does *not*! His affections lie in a different direction.' Marguerite sighed. 'But he must live his own life.'

A pang of anguish shot through Lexa, awakening her to another aspect of the situation. Philippe had hinted that Bryden had 'other plans' for marriage and Lexa's imagination had ranged over other girls in Corsica or even in England. She had not considered Suzanne, who had declared several times that she would win Bryden, and now she had succeeded.

Now Lexa rose, for she knew she must be alone to yield to the wild emotions that surged within her. 'Forgive me, madame, but——' She could manage no more, but walked unsteadily towards the door.

Behind her she heard Marguerite say, 'Do not yet give up hope . . .'

In her own room, Lexa lay on her bed, dry-eyed and stiff with grief. There was nothing to hope for now, she was touching the very depths of despair.

CHAPTER TEN

WHEN three days later Suzanne made a formal call at Fontenay, accompanied by Philippe, Marguerite was clearly affronted.

Suzanne wore a new two-piece of strawberry pink, her

blonde hair framed her face, and her brother had evidently hired a smarter car than his own to honour the occasion.

Most of the conversation was in French, but during the last few months Lexa had improved her knowledge of the language by constantly speaking with Marguerite and Gabrielle, so she understood exactly the polite, but stilted remarks that were exchanged.

'Bryden has not been home for several days,' Marguerite explained, 'so we do not know yet if we are to congratulate him.'

Suzanne was instantly aware of the implied disbelief, but she held her ground. 'When he arrives, madame, he will inform you that he loves me and wishes me to be his wife.'

'I shall wait until I hear that from Bryden himself.' Marguerite's smile was frosty. 'You will understand, Suzanne, that no announcement can be made without his consent.'

'But no, madame, you do not understand. Bryden has already consented by—by taking me as his wife at the inn. We shared a room—the same bed.'

'May I ask which was the inn and where?'

'Naturally. There is only one at San Pietro.'

Lexa closed her eyes in a spasm of momentary relief. At least Bryden had not taken another girl to Calveroso.

'And you made this—this arrangement together?' asked Marguerite.

Suzanne smiled and simpered. 'It was of course his idea.'

Philippe said quickly, 'You will know, madame, of our laws concerning unmarried daughters——'

'Thank you, Philippe, I am well aware of your ancient laws and customs, but this is a matter that concerns Bryden and we shall be guided by what he tells us.'

Philippe jumped to his feet. 'You are not doubting us? There are witnesses! The innkeeper will know who was the man.'

'We shall not need such evidence,' replied Marguerite coldly.

'But I am in honour bound to protect my sister!' declared Philippe.

'Really! Suzanne has been free enough to go where she liked anywhere in the island for quite a long time now.'

'Also, my father will wish to talk with Bryden's father.'

'Then you must arrange such an interview,' answered Marguerite, 'but it must be at a time when Bryden also is here.'

Suzanne decided that it might be wise to leave now. She rose, then curtsied to Marguerite in what Lexa considered an impudent fashion rather than one of humility.

'*Au revoir*, madame.' She leaned forward to kiss Marguerite's cheek, but the latter turned her head away sharply.

But Marguerite rose to accompany Suzanne out on to the terrace, and Lexa was ready to follow suit when Philippe pulled her towards him. 'Now there is no obstacle for us, my darling.'

'There is a very high obstacle between us——'

'No matter. Now that you see Bryden will be my sister's husband, you must let me love you.'

'Never in a thousand years.'

'Perhaps we could even have a double wedding. How marvellous that would be!'

The idea of Lexa's presence at the wedding of Bryden to another girl was surely turning the knife, but she mustered enough composure to say, 'Wedding? Could you saddle yourself with the expense of a *wife*?'

'Oh, there are possibilities,' he replied airily. 'I think I know now how to get some real money. I would be so glad to do that for you.'

'Like robbing a bank? I hope you're not going in for crime, especially on my account.'

Marguerite called from the terrace. 'Philippe! Suzanne is waiting for you to take her home.'

He gave Lexa a brief crushing embrace, kissed her lips and went out to join his sister.

When they had gone, Marguerite sank into a long chair on the terrace. 'I don't know how I kept my temper,' she admitted. 'That girl—quite worthless!'

Gabrielle moved to her mother and put an affectionate arm around her. 'Maman, you were very good—like a marquise in a play, when her son is entangled with a gutter-girl.'

Lexa laughed at that.

'But you will make a formidable mother-in-law,' Gabrielle continued, shivering with mock apprehension. 'I am glad you are my mother.'

'Formidable, perhaps, to Suzanne, but not necessarily to —another girl.'

Lexa caught the brief, straight look that Marguerite flicked at her and was warmed by it.

'And she was so brazen, too,' went on Marguerite. 'Admitting so crudely that she had stayed at the inn.'

A small snippet of information jogged Lexa's memory then. 'The inn at San Pietro belongs to Suzanne's father, so Bryden told me.'

Marguerite nodded a couple of times, but she kept her thoughts to herself and almost immediately went into the house.

After dinner that evening, Edgar showed the nature film for which he had composed the music and he and Lexa did their best to accompany the pictures with sounds on the piano, drums, flute and various other noises imitated by Edgar.

At one point Gabrielle laughed at the antics of a pair of crested cranes bobbing and dancing, so that Lexa lost her next cue, Edgar dropped his steamboat whistle and then had to stop to pick up his drumsticks.

'Gabrielle, you can take your mother's practice cello and thrum a bit here and there,' Edgar instructed. 'That'll keep you from laughing so much and interrupting the performance.'

But by now the film had gone ahead automatically and had to be wound back and started afresh.

'How can I play a cello so that it sounds like a trombone or bassoon?' Gabrielle wanted to know.

'We will use our imagination,' he retorted amiably. 'There are times when you're supposed to be playing a violin and it sounds like a doleful Siamese cat.'

The proceedings became more hilarious as Lexa tried to

keep one eye on the film and the other on the roughly-written score. 'I feel like one of those old-fashioned cinema pianists who played dreamy waltzes for the love scenes and stirring galops for the battlefields.'

At the same time she was glad of this respite from the gnawing anxiety that had been her constant companion ever since she had first heard of Bryden's intention to marry Suzanne.

He came home next day after a protracted visit to the north of the island where he had spent some days in Bastia.

Edgar apparently enlightened him on the situation and some time later, Lexa saw Marguerite strolling with Bryden in the garden. Her arm was linked in his and he appeared to be trying to reassure her.

Before dinner, Gabrielle came bouncing into Lexa's room. 'Bryden says it's not true—about Suzanne.'

Lexa's spirits soared as though a ridiculous thermometer were inside her. 'I'm glad. I knew it couldn't be.'

The subject was not mentioned during the evening meal, but to Lexa's sharp scrutiny Bryden looked worried, or perhaps he was merely tired.

But afterwards he went off in his car and Marguerite told Lexa quietly that he had gone to visit the Morianis. By the time everyone else went to bed, Bryden had not returned, so Lexa had no idea of the outcome of that encounter with Suzanne's father and brother.

Next day, however, the two Morianis, father and son, called at Fontenay and demanded to see both Edgar and Bryden. Evidently a stormy interview took place between the four men in Edgar's study.

Eventually Gregorio emerged, using what appeared to be threatening and abusive language for he was speaking in the Corsican dialect. Lexa and Gabrielle had just come downstairs and were in the hall. Edgar replied in French that threats and blackmail would do neither Gregorio nor Suzanne any good and ushered out his unwelcome guest.

Lexa and Gabrielle thought it more discreet to move away from the scene of conflict, but Lexa heard Philippe say to Bryden, 'That piece of land you wanted up at Calveroso —I know who owns it—and I could get it for you at a cheap price.'

Bryden's reply was curt. 'I can do without your bribes.'

Lexa disappeared swiftly in the direction of the kitchen to evade Philippe. She was not at all in the mood for his admiring advances.

Some time afterwards Bryden was discussing the whole affair with his father and Marguerite. Lexa had risen to leave, not wishing to intrude on a family matter, but Bryden told her to remain.

'It's a complete tissue of lies!' Bryden asserted. 'I went to San Pietro a few days ago, but I stayed only a couple of hours in the morning. There was no sign of Suzanne or Gregorio Moriani then. The innkeeper says that I came back in the evening and stayed two nights with Suzanne. Of course, he's been bribed——'

'It might be possible to bribe him to change his tale,' suggested Edgar.

'Not likely!' Bryden's voice rose in anger. 'I'm not stooping to their damned dirty tricks. They can do what they like —*vendetta* or anything else they can think up, but I'm not falling for this nasty little plot. Suzanne will have to look elsewhere.'

Lexa was overjoyed to find Bryden in this frame of mind.

'As to that piece of land I wanted at Calveroso, I'd already found out who owned it while I was up there. As you might guess, Moriani the elder. He bought it only recently because he had wind of the fact that I was interested in the small inn there and would need the land to enlarge the place. Philippe offered to get it for me cheap!'

For the next few days Lexa saw little of Bryden, for he was away most of the time, but the household seemed to have settled down to a reasonable harmony. There were no further visits from Philippe or Suzanne.

Then one evening Bryden returned home with the news that someone had slashed his car tyres when he was at one of the inns he and his father owned.

'All four of them,' he said bitterly. 'Made a proper job of it.'

Two days later he reported that he had met a flock of sheep on the road, waited patiently while they were driven by and then the shepherd had accused him of killing one of the sheep.

'It was ludicrous! I asked where was the carcase, then, but he gave a cackling laugh and said he would show that to the police.'

'How could he do that?' asked Marguerite.

'Simple. He'll kill a sheep—to use it for mutton—then claim that was the one I ran into.'

'This is the *vendetta* that Moriani threatened,' said Marguerite with a nervous shiver. 'Do be careful, Bryden.'

'Of course. Not to worry.'

But in the following weeks there were other incidents not only concerning Bryden, but the rest of the family as well.

Edgar was walking in the woods one day when two young men seemed to be playing carelessly with shotguns and a bullet came dangerously close to Edgar's head. A large stone was thrown through the windscreen as Marguerite and Edgar were driving home from Sartène. Gabrielle received a box containing what looked like a child's toy, but turned out to be an ingenious gadget for trapping the hands of violinists. Gabrielle rescued her precious fingers just in time.

Lexa seemed the only one who was immune until the day she was walking down towards the tiny village on the shore near Fontenay. A small van and a motor-bike came clattering down the road, the motor-cyclist swerved towards her so that she had to jump for safety into the bushes bordering the track.

'Roadhog!' she muttered, as she resumed walking, then was astounded when the cyclist came up again towards her, driving straight at her, so that this time she had to fling herself into the bushes. After that she waited for some time in case he came back for another go. There was no further sound and she started again and was within sight of the

173

few dwellings and the beach café when the van came roaring uphill. As it passed within inches of her, she tried to see the driver, but he was wearing dark glasses and an old straw hat pulled down over his face.

But the incident had scared Lexa, so that she gave up one of her favourite walks and remained within the boundary of the Fontenay house, except when she walked down to the small beach to swim.

So this was the way the *vendetta* worked. First, the small harrying incidents, then perhaps something more violent. Every day when Bryden was away in some other part of the island, Lexa feared for his safety, but realised there was nothing she could do about it.

One announcement, however, cheered her. Gabrielle came back from Sartène one day after her master class and said resignedly, 'I've finished with Stefano.'

'Good,' commented Lexa. 'But any particular incident?'

'He likes too many girls. In Propriano—even in Sartène. I found he was meeting one of the other girls at the class. She lives in Sartène and met him on other days. Then there was yourself. Oh, he never stopped asking me about you.'

'So you decided he was not worth bothering about?'

'I told him I was going to Paris soon.' Gabrielle turned round swiftly towards Lexa. 'Do you know what he said? That he would wave me goodbye at the airport and also soon he would go back to Naples, so we would have to part anyway. Imagine! So cool! So calm! If he had loved me he would tear his hair, kneel at my feet, beg me to stay, or else he would follow me to Paris. So let him have all his other girls.'

Now it was September and Lexa watched the chestnut trees turning gold, then to burnt sienna. When the chestnuts had been gathered in oval baskets, then loaded into sacks for the donkeys, and the leaves had fluttered down, she would be on her way home again, for Gabrielle would have left for Paris.

'Why don't we go to the Niolo Fair?' suggested Marguerite. 'Lexa hasn't had much chance of seeing any of the local events since she's been here.'

Edgar agreed it was a good idea. 'I think it might be better to try to stay at one of the Corte hotels. Those at Calacuccia will be full, I think.'

Marguerite shrugged. 'Anywhere, so long as it's clean and the beds are not too hard.' She smiled at her husband. 'As one of the island's leading hoteliers, you should be able to ensure that.'

'Perhaps we will buy an inn specially for you, *chérie*, in every region of the island.'

The three-day Fair was an event that Lexa would always remember. The religious festival on the first day, with a miraculous statue of the Virgin—'*la Santa*' carried in procession from the church to the fairground; next day the best mountain singers congregating to take part in competitions. Edgar and Marguerite helped Lexa to understand the improvised songs and the sung dialogues that made up this remarkable festival of archaic music and verse.

The melancholy airs were accompanied by guitars or zithers, pipes and sometimes Jew's harp, and seemed to reflect the sorrows and griefs of the Corsican past.

But there were also lively scenes around the fairground booths, which sold everything from food to clothing, wines and souvenirs. There were markets for horses, donkeys and mules, and Lexa noticed that most of the shepherds and other men were tall and fair.

'Different from most of the Corsican locals,' she remarked.

'Mostly nomads,' replied Bryden. 'They graze their flocks up here in the summer, but the Niolo is snow-capped for about seven or eight months in the year, so they drive the flocks down to the coasts for the winter.' After a pause, he continued, 'It's well known here that it's always a female sheep who leads the herds and flocks of animals over ranges, through forests, across rivers sometimes, and the shepherds allow her to choose the route.'

Bryden had joined the party only today, the last day of the fair, and Lexa was delighted to have his company, even for a few hours, although his nearness did nothing to calm her jumpy emotions.

Driving home in the Corsican twilight and sitting next to him was a mixed blessing and when on one occasion his right arm touched her shoulder, she experienced again that wild, ecstatic thrill that always swept over her.

They were almost home when a cloud of smoke drifted across the road and Bryden slowed down.

'It's a fire somewhere,' he said. Then, 'Good God! It's the Moriani place.'

He was out of the car and disappeared into the smoke in a matter of a few seconds. Edgar followed more slowly, leaving Marguerite and Lexa in the car.

Lexa knew now with a sinking heart that the real truth had been shown to her. Bryden really loved Suzanne and he was fearful about her safety.

'I must go and see if I can help,' Lexa muttered now to Marguerite, and followed the men.

The house was blazing like tinder and in the light of the flames Lexa saw Gregorio Moriani looking more like a bandit than ever. He was appealing to Bryden and Edgar for help, apparently, but it seemed there was not much to be done, for the water supply had failed.

Lexa stood watching, irritated by the sight of three men calmly watching a house burn down.

Then suddenly Suzanne appeared, bundles of clothes in her hands. 'Take these,' she said to Lexa. 'I must bring the others. My lovely dresses.'

Before Lexa could stop her, Suzanne had rushed back into the ground floor of the house. 'Suzanne! Suzanne! Come back!'

Then it was that Bryden rushed across to Lexa.

'Save Suzanne!' she shouted. 'She's gone back inside.'

But, although Lexa was now appalled at the danger to Bryden as well as Suzanne, she was astonished to see him approach Gregorio and begin an angry conversation. The old Corsican clasped his hands in supplication, but Bryden still held the man's arm and continued to shout in dialect.

'Bryden!' Lexa was unable to stand any more of this pantomime while a girl might be suffocated in the burning house.

With his free arm, Bryden waved her aside, then as he saw her run towards the house, he pulled her roughly away.

'Don't be a fool! Leave it to me! I know what I'm doing.'

Gregorio had fallen to his knees as the flames shot through the roof of the house.

'Stay there!' ordered Bryden. 'I'm going round the back.'

A few moments later he emerged again into the fire's reflection, accompanied by Suzanne and Edgar.

'Take Suzanne to the car, Lexa,' he commanded. 'The *maquis* is catching alight and we must warn the Gendarmerie. I'll stay here and cope if I can. My father will drive back to Sartène first.'

Marguerite helped Suzanne into the car, along with the armfuls of clothing she had managed to save, but the girl was very subdued, obviously from shock.

'How did it happen?' asked Marguerite after a few minutes.

'My father—was in the yard, then he went into the shed —the paint was there—and I suppose his cigar fell into it, and started a blaze.'

It was not until Bryden arrived home in the early hours of the morning that the full story could be pieced together.

Edgar had been outside from time to time watching to see if the *maquis* fire had been put out or was spreading up into the hills.

'Trouble is it smoulders, then flashes up next day,' he said.

Bryden arrived with his face blackened, his clothes dirty and torn, but there was a triumphant light in his eyes.

'A pity about the fire,' he said to his father, 'but we've managed to fix the old man.'

Lexa and Marguerite had stayed up because they were too anxious about Bryden's safety to go to bed, but Suzanne had been given a room and had evidently fallen into an exhausted sleep.

'I'll tell you about it in the morning,' Bryden promised.

'No, tell us now!' demanded Marguerite. 'We've waited long enough. Five minutes more before you can reach a bathroom will be enough.'

'I—well, I bargained with old Moriani. I'd rescue Suzanne if he'd agree to call off his *vendetta* and stop this silly nonsense about marrying her because I was supposed to have been at one of his inns.'

Lexa's mouth opened in horrified amazement. 'Bryden! How *could* you? Suzanne might have been——'

Bryden held up a grimy hand. 'Suzanne was quite safe. Father was holding her outside the back door, but old Moriani didn't know that. So I blackmailed him into agreeing my terms and made sure that Suzanne heard him, too.'

'Do you think he'll abide by what he promised?' queried Marguerite.

'As a Corsican, he must, I think. He swore on the sacred head of his daughter that he knew I'd never been near the inn and that he bribed the innkeeper to say I had. He even offered to give me free of charge that piece of land at Calveroso which he owns and knows I want, but I told him I'd give him a fair price for it.'

Lexa said thoughtfully, 'I wonder where Philippe was. If he'd been at home he could probably have helped them save some of their possessions.'

Bryden's face instantly changed. He had been smiling in a happy, though tired, way. Now he said brusquely, 'I doubt if you need worry about Philippe. He has interests that keep him in Ajaccio and other places sometimes.'

He walked away out of the room, no doubt longing for a bath and a sleep.

When Lexa saw Suzanne next morning she was shocked by the change in the girl.

'Monsieur Frankland offered to drive me down to our house and see what can be saved, but I refused.' Suzanne spoke in a dejected voice. 'All I wanted were my dresses and other clothes.'

'But you've rescued some of those,' pointed out Lexa, indicating the half dozen dresses laid on one of the chairs.

'There were more, but Monsieur Frankland would not let me go upstairs and get them.'

'But your life was in danger. You might have been burned or suffocated, and then what good would the dresses be?'

Suzanne shrugged mournfully. 'Some of them were for one of the shops in Ajaccio. But nothing matters now. I heard my father agree not to continue the *vendetta* against Bryden and his family. Also, I heard him swear that he would not insist on Bryden marrying me.'

'But, Suzanne dear, you must admit that was all a put-up job.'

'What else? Bryden will never look at me with love in his eyes. Since you came he has eyes only for you.'

'You're mistaken!' exclaimed Lexa.

'Oh, I was so jealous of you, Lexa. I had to think of ways to get rid of you or at least make you go back to England.'

The incident at the swimming party came instantly to Lexa's mind. 'You mean when—someone—tried to hold me down in the water that night in Ajaccio when we all went swimming?'

'It was not a good idea,' murmured Suzanne.

'Where will you go now? Madame Frankland would let you stay until——'

'Oh, no! I am partly Corsican and I have pride! My father and I will go to our relatives in Zonza or Olmeto.'

Marguerite naturally offered hospitality to Suzanne for any indefinite period, but the girl refused with appealing dignity.

'Thank you, madame, but it is best that I go immediately.'

Edgar drove the girl down later in the day to the wrecked house, collected Gregorio Moriani and took the pair to Olmeto.

When Gabrielle arrived home next day from a few days' visit to friends in Ajaccio, she was chagrined to have missed all the excitement, but delighted that Suzanne would not be so near a neighbour.

'So Bryden is free at last!' she exclaimed happily. 'Such a stupid plot! He would never marry Suzanne in a thousand years.'

A week later Gabrielle left for Paris with her mother who had already arranged where her daughter was to stay during her tuition at the Paris Conservatoire. Lexa now had all

179

her time to concentrate on score-copying for Edgar, in particular his new cello concerto for Marguerite.

One afternoon when they were working together, he said, 'Lexa, have you thought about staying on here? Indefinitely, I mean. You could make your home with us and Marguerite and I would be charmed.' •

'It's very kind of you,' she replied, near to tears at the generosity of his invitation. 'But I'd rather go back on the date when I arranged.'

He sighed. 'I shall miss you, Lexa, but in any case, we shall meet when I come to London next spring for the concerts.'

Better leave it at that, she thought. How could she bear to stay on at Fontenay, knowing that Bryden, in spite of Suzanne's opinion, would never look at her with love in his eyes? Somewhere in Corsica, or even in England, there was another girl for whom that rapture was reserved.

Since the fire at the Morianis' Bryden had been away even more than usual. One night he came home and discussed with his father the probable cause of the fire.

'Of course, they weren't insured!' he said angrily. 'I went down there specially with an insurance man from Ajaccio, to try to sort out some compensation for the old man. But nothing doing. The old fool had dropped the butt end of a cigar into an opened tin of paint and when it caught fire, he panicked and kicked over a can of paraffin. So of course the whole shoot went up. So old, it burned like matchwood.'

Lexa listening quietly at the other end of the room felt a jab of guilt. It had been her idea to persuade Philippe and Suzanne to paint up the house, but then it was possible that the fire would have happened without the paint.

'What happened to the housekeeper there, Blanche?' she asked.

'She was out somewhere at the time, came home and saw the wreck and promptly disappeared,' Edgar answered. 'Probably stayed with relatives.'

Next day Edgar went to the airport to meet a friend and for the first time Bryden and Lexa were the only members of the household at dinner.

By sheer chance Lexa had put on the elegant dress that Suzanne had made for the recital in Ajaccio, and when Bryden remarked on how well it suited her, her cheeks went pink with pleasure.

'Suzanne is a clever needlewoman,' she murmured.

After that moment there seemed to her to be a kind of electric thrill in the air, a sense of expectation, a rose-coloured anticipation. She was glad that she was sitting opposite to him and there was no possibility of an accidental contact, unless of course he stretched out his hand across the table.

'Too cold outside for our coffee?' he queried when Sophie, the housekeeper, cleared the remaining dishes.

'Oh, no. The evenings are still warm,' she replied.

For some time after they had both finished their coffee they sat on the darkened terrace with the fragrance of the garden flowers and shrubs under a starlit sky providing an aura of restful peace. Yet there was no peace in Lexa's heart, for she guessed that she was on the threshold of either a few moments of that longed-for bliss that had so far eluded her, or she would be plunged into an abyss of heartache.

'I—er—bought you a box, Lexa,' Bryden said at last. 'One of those plaited chestnut wood things that you admired when we were up in the mountains.'

'But you insisted on giving me that other one. You wouldn't let me pay for it.' She remembered the scene when she had offered him the money and he had refused. 'Keep it as a souvenir. You can put your love-letters in it,' he had suggested.

Now from somewhere behind him he produced a parcel and put it on the table in front of her.

As she undid the wrappings she tried to smile. 'Another souvenir?' she queried, her lips trembling.

'Perhaps. I didn't quite know what else to give you.'

But you do know! her mind clamoured. *I want your love, not boxes I can buy for myself.*

'Thank you very much.' In the subdued light from the corner lantern that shone dimly across the table she could see that the box was a most handsome one, with a satin-lined tray and drawers that pulled out. It would hold a quantity of love-letters, she thought bitterly.

Then without warning he rose to his feet and pulled her into his arms. 'Lexa, my love.' He was kissing her with the rapturous intensity she had dreamed of and she returned his kisses and held him close to her as his lips sought the hollow of her neck. Her chin rested on his thick brown hair and she felt her own soft body moulded against his masculine strength.

Then he tilted her chin with his fingers. 'I wish it could be otherwise . . . I thought you might be the one girl for me, but—oh, how can I say it? I'm no use to any woman. I bring them bad luck . . . I couldn't let you trust your life to me.'

She drew away from him in consternation. 'Bryden! What are you saying?'

Now he held her elbows in a sinewy grip. 'It's evidently not my fate to—marry.'

The enchantment of the moment had vanished, giving place to anger. 'That's cowardly!' she accused. 'Because you've had previous bad experiences——' she broke off. Then, in a whisper, she asked, 'Don't you believe in love?'

'Love?' he echoed. 'I wonder——'

'But, Bryden my darling, I love you with all my heart. Together we could——'

'I've loved you—for a long time now. I fought against it, knowing what happened to those other two girls. But now I must fight even more. Go back to England and forget me. Marry Clifford and be happy.'

She was too shaken by despair to tell him that a week ago a letter from Aunt Beatrice had told her that Clifford had recently announced his engagement to a local girl.

His hands dropped to his sides and she stood there facing him, only a few inches separating her from him but inches that were the widest possible chasm of desolation.

'It might have been,' he was saying in a low, tense voice, 'better if we'd never met.'

'I didn't realise you were such a coward,' she replied. 'It would certainly have been better for me—if I'd never known you.'

She turned away slowly and moved towards the french windows that led indoors. If only he would take her in his arms again, kiss her, tell her that he loved her and would never let her go! But he was leaning over the stone balustrade of the terrace, as she saw when she glanced over her shoulder. Physically and symbolically he had turned his back on her.

As she mounted the stairs to her bedroom, she cried out in silent anguish that this was surely the cruellest blow that any man could deal to a girl who loved him. To tempt her to a full revelation of her desire, to show her a brief glimpse of paradise, then to snatch away the fulfilment. Bryden certainly knew how to twist the knife and now, for the first time, Lexa wondered if those previous girls had been promised heaven and then denied it.

She was glad when at last the day came to fly home. Edgar and Marguerite accompanied her to the airport and she was relieved that Bryden was not with them. In fact, she had not even seen him since the night when he had given her the chestnut wood box but withheld his love.

'If you change your mind, Lexa,' Edgar was saying, 'we'll be glad to welcome you back. In any case, we shall see you in February.'

At the last goodbye, Marguerite embraced Lexa with warm affection and kissed her on both cheeks. 'You *will* come back to us. I know,' she asserted firmly.

When the plane took off, Lexa fancied she could see Bryden among the spectators waving to passengers, but no doubt she was imagining Bryden in almost every man she saw. Corsica was far behind when her self-control collapsed and the first slow tears fell down her cheeks as she said farewell to a dream.

Aunt Beatrice gave her the warmest welcome, telling her all the news of the neighbourhood. 'I think I did mention about Clifford? I hope his engagement didn't upset you?'

Lexa shook her head. 'Not in the least. I'm very glad. I hope he'll be happy.'

In due course she was shown the various small improvements her aunt had made in the house. 'It was very good of you to send home the money from time to time. Look, I threw out that old settee and bought these two new chairs instead.'

During the winter months Lexa shut out memories of Corsica and concentrated on the new job she had found as a school secretary. It might be only temporary, she had been warned, while the usual secretary was ill, but Lexa was content not to look too far ahead into the future.

During the Christmas holidays she met Clifford, accompanied by his fiancée, a pretty girl whom Lexa knew slightly.

'No hard feelings?' queried Clifford when there was a quiet moment alone together.

'None at all, Clifford,' she answered sincerely. 'I do wish both of you complete happiness.'

'And you? I thought you'd settle for either of those two chaps in Corsica—probably the French one.'

She smiled and shook her head. 'No attachments of that kind.'

In February she received the tickets for Edgar's concert at the Festival Hall. Lexa was torn in two. To see Edgar and Marguerite again would revive all that intolerable longing for Bryden, a longing which she was trying hard to crush out of her existence. Yet the Franklands had been so kind to her, it would be churlish not to attend the concert, apart from depriving Aunt Beatrice of a musical treat.

'I've never been to the *première* of a concerto before,' she had said happily before debating on what she would wear.

Lexa chose the cream and bronze dress that Suzanne had made. It was still one of her nicest dresses and she saw no reason not to wear it, even if it reminded her of those 'old unhappy far-off things'.

Only a few minutes before the overture *The Corsair*, the seat next to Lexa was unoccupied and involuntarily her thoughts flew to Bryden. But it was Gabrielle who slipped quietly into the seat.

184

'Just in time!' she whispered. 'It was difficult for me to get special week-end leave from Paris, but I flew in this afternoon.'

At the end of the overture, Lexa eagerly awaited the new cello concerto and joined in the applause when Edgar, who was guest conductor for his new work, led on the soloist, his wife, Marguerite, wearing a most lovely gown of shimmering amethyst silk.

The orchestra began the opening theme, so well known to Lexa, who had written down every note of the score. Then the entry of the soloist, and the imaginative transformations of melody with a rich texture of harmony. The Adagio second movement Lexa especially liked, with its haunting air that was almost a lament, and then the finale taken up by horns and woodwind, with the strings dying away to give place to the soloist again, and a final blaze of sound to make a most satisfying close.

The applause was tremendous and Marguerite was recalled over and over again.

'Your father must be very pleased at the reception of his new work,' Lexa said to Gabrielle.

'Perhaps one day he will write a violin concerto for me, but I doubt whether I shall ever be such a great artist as Maman.'

The second half of the concert was devoted to a Sibelius symphony, the Second, and Lexa relaxed to drink in the glorious sound of the instruments, one section answering another, until the finale was almost too much to bear with its climbing chords and impressive harmonies.

The roaring applause around her at the end left her still rather dazed as she and Gabrielle, with Aunt Beatrice eventually moved out of the concert hall.

'My mother asked me to bring you both to the room where she has been resting,' said Gabrielle, guiding the other two along a corridor and through an open door.

Edgar and Marguerite with a few other people were relaxing and Lexa introduced her aunt to them both.

Edgar grasped Lexa's hands. 'I owe you a great deal, my dear Lexa. Without your help, that score of mine would never have been ready in time.'

In turn, Lexa congratulated Marguerite on her splendid performance.

'We must wait for the verdict of the critics,' replied Marguerite, 'before we know whether we have a success or not.' Then she beckoned Lexa nearer to her. 'Someone is outside with some flowers for you.'

'For me?'

'Yes. Will you go and take them?'

Lexa supposed that Edgar had probably arranged for the flowers, but when she stepped into the corridor, there was Bryden holding a delicious bouquet of carnations and roses.

She tried to draw back into the room she had just left, but his arm had gone around her waist and he was gently propelling her towards the end of the corridor.

'Will you forgive me, Lexa?' he murmured huskily.

All her love for him surged up as never before, but she forced herself to be hard. 'Not another spell of blowing hot and cold, please, Bryden.'

'Nothing cold about me now,' he said. 'I haven't had a moment's peace since the day I let you go, when I saw your plane take you away. I was ten thousand times a fool, but it was because I had no faith in myself.'

'Nor in me?' she queried.

'Perhaps not enough in you. But I know now that wherever you are, I must be there—that is, if you'll let me,' he added humbly. 'You were right. I was a coward, as Marguerite told me a dozen times.'

By now he had piloted her out into the street and towards the parapet that ran alongside the Thames.

Trains rumbled over Hungerford Bridge, across the river the floodlit buildings resembled stage sets and were reflected in the dark flowing tide. A police patrol boat chugged downstream to where St Paul's was bathed in light and here in the shadows Lexa was held close to this man who had captured her heart, but yet managed to reward her with so much pain and heartache. So few people were now about that she and Bryden might have been entirely alone wrapped in a world of their own.

'Are you sure?' she asked tremulously. 'I want all of you, Bryden, not just the part of you left over from—from those previous tragic affairs.'

'My darling, they had sad endings, but ours, I promise you, shall have no ending at all, only joy and happiness for ever.'

For a long time they stood together, their two outlines melting into one, while he kissed her lips, her cheeks, her eyes, her hair, and she responded as to no other man and never would, even if she lived to be ninety.

'You haven't said what I want to hear,' she said softly, her arms still entwined around his neck.

'You first. Ladies first, naturally.'

'Oh, I do love you, Bryden. I'll always love you.'

'My lovely, I can't begin to tell you how much I love you. But come on, you'll be getting cold and I must take care of you from now on.'

But she was far from chilled, for she was wearing a short fur jacket over her dress and even apart from that, Bryden's love was enough to warm even the most frigid girl.

He called a passing taxi and as she stepped into it, she cried out, 'The flowers! My bouquet!'

He dashed back and rescued the cellophane-wrapped blooms and handed them to her.

'Where are we going?' she asked.

'For a small celebration on our own. My father and Marguerite and all the rest of them are having a supper party at the Savoy, but I'll take you to a small place I know in Soho, where we'll drink champagne and enrage the waiters by letting our food get cold, and we'll tell each other our life stories.'

But there were a few more details that Lexa would like to know. She waited until they were halfway through the meal. Then she put her hand in his and said gently, 'Bryden, tell me about those other girls—if it doesn't hurt you too much.'

'Until now, I think it has always hurt me to think I might have been responsible, but—well, Catherine, my first fiancée, just fell out of love with me and in with another man. I wish she had been honest enough to tell me, but she went off to Paris with the other man and I think you know that they were both killed when the small plane crashed, and the pilot with them. Three lives wasted.'

He paused and a spasm of pain crossed his face. 'Veronica was young, twenty, I think, and wanted to be a sophisticated *femme fatale*. She thought it was clever to try to have half a dozen men begging for her favours. Actually, we were not definitely engaged, but when it pleased her, she'd refer to me as her fiancé. She began to drink heavily and on the night of the swimming party, she had certainly drunk too much. I tried to reason with her, tell her it was madness to go bathing, but she eluded me and the next thing I knew they were bringing her out of the water.'

He lifted his champagne glass towards her, his eyes sparkling again. 'Third time lucky!' he whispered, clinking his glass with hers.

After a while he said, 'What about you and Philippe? I began to wonder what chance I had with that Don Juan.'

'Don Juan? Surely not as notorious as that!'

He leaned forward. 'I didn't tell you, but I knew that Philippe shared a small flat sometimes in Ajaccio with another chap—and he took girls there.'

Lexa smiled. 'It was Philippe who never had a chance with me.'

'Then Stefano. Why didn't you tell me that he was really Gaby's friend?'

'How could I let her down? It was only a young girl's crush and I knew it wouldn't last, but I had to protect her if I could. How did you know?'

Bryden smiled. 'Gaby told me herself. I ought to have known how loyal you'd be, but I was so furious when I thought he was one of your admirers that I wanted to take the man by the neck and throttle him.'

'And Suzanne? What has happened to her?' asked Lexa.

'She's married and living in Nice. She went there with Philippe and met this well-to-do Frenchman, so she settled for him right away.'

'I'm glad. I hope she'll be very happy.' Lexa spared a

passing sympathetic thought for the girl who had imagined herself in love with Bryden and gone to such lengths to secure him. Perhaps, after all, Suzanne needed a comfortable home, an escape from the dilapidated shack that was now only a few scorched walls after the fire.

But Bryden was holding her hand and telling her of the future. 'You must come back to Corsica with us, or the moment you can. I'm certainly not going without you. It's still February and you'll see the "white spring" when the almond blossom covers the island like snow. Then there's the white heath and cherry, plum, pear, peach and the white asphodels. You didn't come early enough last year to see the spring, but now you'll be there to see all the seasons, all the festivals.'

'One long holiday!' she put in delightedly.

'I shall take up my architecture practice again in England and we'll have a house here, wherever you want, and another in Corsica, for I shall still have to look after my father's interests. Left to himself, his finances would soon slide downhill.'

'Indispensable Bryden!' she teased.

'Indispensable to you?'

'Essential and irreplaceable,' she answered. Suddenly she remembered. 'Aunt Beatrice! I've left her in the lurch.'

'No, you haven't. My father and Marguerite are taking care of her, giving her a night out at the Savoy. We'll go there and join them when we're ready.'

They left the restaurant. 'My flowers!' Lexa exclaimed.

Dutifully, Bryden retrieved them. 'The fetch-and-carry man, that's what I am.'

She laughed delightedly. Then she paused to glance at the card attached to the sheaf of flowers. In the light of a shopwindow she read, 'To Lexa, with all my love, Bryden.'

She reached up and planted a kiss on the side of his chin. 'Bless you, Bryden.'

But she knew it was she herself who was blessed for she had gained his precious, unfaltering love for always.

Did you miss any of these exciting Harlequin Omnibus 3-in-1 volumes?

Each volume contains 3 great novels by one author for only $1.95.
See order coupon.

Violet Winspear

Violet Winspear #3
The Cazalet Bride (#1434)
Beloved Castaway (#1472)
The Castle of the Seven Lilacs (#1514)

Anne Mather

Anne Mather
Charlotte's Hurricane (#1487)
Lord of Zaracus (#1574)
The Reluctant Governess (#1600)

Anne Hampson

Anne Hampson #1
Unwary Heart (#1388)
Precious Waif (#1420)
The Autocrat of Melhurst (#1442)

Betty Neels

Betty Neels
Tempestuous April (#1441)
Damsel in Green (#1465)
Tulips for Augusta (#1529)

Essie Summers

Essie Summers #3
Summer in December (#1416)
The Bay of the Nightingales (#1445)
Return to Dragonshill (#1502)

Margaret Way

Margaret Way
King Country (#1470)
Blaze of Silk (#1500)
The Man from Bahl Bahla (#1530)

Available only by mail!

40 magnificent Omnibus volumes to choose from:

Essie Summers #1
Bride in Flight (#933)
Postscript to Yesterday
(#1119)
Meet on My Ground
(#1326)

Jean S. MacLeod
The Wolf of Heimra
(#990)
Summer Island (#1314)
Slave of the Wind
(#1339)

Eleanor Farnes
The Red Cliffs (#1335)
The Flight of the Swan
(#1280)
Sister of the
Housemaster (#975)

Susan Barrie #1
Marry a Stranger
(#1034)
Rose in the Bud (#1168)
The Marriage Wheel
(#1311)

Violet Winspear #1
Beloved Tyrant (#1032)
Court of the Veils
(#1267)
Palace of the Peacocks
(#1318)

Isobel Chace
The Saffron Sky
(#1250)
A Handful of Silver
(#1306)
The Damask Rose
(#1334)

Joyce Dingwell #1
Will You Surrender
(#1179)
A Taste for Love
(#1229)
The Feel of Silk (#1342)

Sara Seale
Queen of Hearts
(#1324)
Penny Plain (#1197)
Green Girl (#1045)

Jane Arbor
A Girl Named Smith
(#1000)
Kingfisher Tide (#950)
The Cypress Garden
(#1336)

Anne Weale
The Sea Waif (#1123)
The Feast of Sara
(#1007)
Doctor in Malaya (#914)

Essie Summers #2
His Serene Miss Smith
(#1093)
The Master to Tawhai
(#910)
A Place Called Paradise
(#1156)

Catherine Airlie
Doctor Overboard
(#979)
Nobody's Child (#1258)
A Wind Sighing (#1328)

Violet Winspear #2
Bride's Dilemma
(#1008)
Tender Is the Tyrant
(#1208)
The Dangerous Delight
(#1344)

Kathryn Blair
Doctor Westland (#954)
Battle of Love (#1038)
Flowering Wilderness
(#1148)

Rosalind Brett
The Girl at White Drift
(#1101)
Winds of Enchantment
(#1176)
Brittle Bondage (#1319)

Rose Burghley
Man of Destiny (#960)
The Sweet Surrender
(#1023)
The Bay of Moonlight
(#1245)

Iris Danbury
Rendezvous in Lisbon
(#1178)
Doctor at Villa Ronda
(#1257)
Hotel Belvedere (#1331)

Amanda Doyle
A Change for Clancy
(#1085)
Play the Tune Softly
(#1116)
A Mist in Glen Torran
(#1308)

Great value in Reading!
Use the handy order form

Elizabeth Hoy
Snare the Wild Heart (#992)
The Faithless One (#1104)
Be More than Dreams (#1286)

Roumelia Lane
House of the Winds (#1262)
A Summer to Love (#1280)
Sea of Zanj (#1338)

Margaret Malcolm
The Master of Normanhurst (#1028)
The Man in Homespun (#1140)
Meadowsweet (#1164)

Joyce Dingwell #2
The Timber Man (#917)
Project Sweetheart (#964)
Greenfingers Farm (#999)

Marjorie Norell
Nurse Madeline of Eden Grove (#962)
Thank You, Nurse Conway (#1097)
The Marriage of Doctor Royle (#1177)

Anne Durham
New Doctor at Northmoor (#1242)
Nurse Sally's Last Chance (#1281)
Mann of the Medical Wing (#1313)

Henrietta Reid
Reluctant Masquerade (#1380)
Hunter's Moon (#1430)
The Black Delaney (#1460)

Lucy Gillen
The Silver Fishes (#1408)
Heir to Glen Ghyll (#1450)
The Girl at Smuggler's Rest (#1533)

Anne Hampson #2
When the Bough Breaks (#1491)
Love Hath an Island (#1522)
Stars of Spring (#1551)

Essie Summers #4
No Legacy for Lindsay (#957)
No Orchids by Request (#982)
Sweet Are the Ways (#1015)

Mary Burchell #3
The Other Linding Girl (#1431)
Girl with a Challenge (#1455)
My Sister Celia (#1474)

Susan Barrie #2
Return to Tremarth (#1359)
Night of the Singing Birds (#1428)
Bride in Waiting (#1526)

Violet Winspear #4
Desert Doctor (#921)
The Viking Stranger (#1080)
The Tower of the Captive (#1111)

Essie Summers #5
Heir to Windrush Hill (#1055)
Rosalind Comes Home (#1283)
Revolt — and Virginia (#1348)

Doris E. Smith
To Sing Me Home (#1427)
Seven of Magpies (#1454)
Dear Deceiver (#1599)

Katrina Britt
Healer of Hearts (#1393)
The Fabulous Island (#1490)
A Spray of Edelweiss (#1626)

Betty Neels #2
Sister Peters in Amsterdam (#1361)
Nurse in Holland (#1385)
Blow Hot — Blow Cold (#1409)

Amanda Doyle #2
The Girl for Gillgong (#1351)
The Year at Yattabilla (#1448)
Kookaburra Dawn (#1562)